MURDER & THE HEIR

A Violet Carlyle Historical Mystery Book 1

BETH BYERS

For Mumma. In a book about near-mothers, I can't help but think of my own near-perfect mother. I love you, babe.

SUMMARY

Violet Carlyle--along with a slew of relatives--is called to spend the holidays with their aunt, Agatha Davies. The intransigent woman has spent the majority of her life squirreling away money and alienating her family.

It's hardly the first time Vi has spent the holidays with her aunt. She and her twin intend to do what they always do. Enjoy Aunt Aggie's luxuries while ignoring the histrionics of the family trying to worm their way into the will.

Only this time, Aunt Aggie claims someone is trying to kill her. But how can that be true? Before Vi can find the killer, Aunt Aggie dies. Since Agatha never named an heir, why would anyone want to kill her?

To her shock, Vi finds herself embroiled in a murder investigation where she and her family are the suspects. Just who murdered Aunt Agatha? And why? Will they be able to find the killer before someone else dies?

NOTE

This book is written in American English. For my British friends, I appreciate your patience with our differences.

CHAPTER ONE

"*D*o you really have an appointment so early, Vi?"

"Indeed, dear one," she said, taking the two pills from Giles and the rather noxious concoction that should shake the last of her after-effects from the previous evening.

"We have a letter from Aunt Agatha," Vic told her with a bit of a plea.

"It is your turn to answer for us, darling," Vi said, "I have to deal with our stepmother. She offered me a few things I needed for my wardrobe along with a dress for some party she'll expect me to do the pretty at while I attend and pretend to be good."

"Ahhh, she's persuaded some bloke to *take* a look at you," he laughed.

Violet took up the concoction, drained it in several swallows, and shuddered. Her brother, spoiled soul that he was, never suffered from overindulgence. As his twin, she objected strenuously.

"Must you, darling? I am always certain whenever I answer Aunt Agatha that I've been cross-examined and found wanting."

"Dearest darling," Vi said, taking up her teacup as though it were from the gods' own table, "Stepmother is far easier to deal with if you

1

give her what she wants when it doesn't matter and slip away at the opportune moment. Better to feed the bear than to make her rabid."

"I don't think you become rabid from not eating," Vic mused, filling his plate with kedgeree and toast.

Violet shuddered and pushed the kedgeree farther away her. "Perhaps not. I am not quite up to verbally sparring yet, luv."

"Well, I'll deal with Aggie and see you here for tea? I have dinner plans with Martha Landsy. Would you like to come?"

"I have dinner plans of my own, Victor dear. I'll see what the old battle axe has planned for you, shall I? Then perhaps we should look at escaping London after the New Year and before Stepmother gets too many plans in the works."

"Running scared from the fella ready to give you the look over?"

"There's no shame in a well thought out retreat."

Buying dresses with her stepmother was exactly what Vi thought it would be. She was told that she was getting too old to expect anyone to marry her and she couldn't expect Victor to support her forever. As though Vi didn't contribute to their rooms and living. If her stepmother only knew half the truth, she might leave Violet be, but Vi believed in keeping her cards close to her chest.

"I can only do so much for you, Violet," the battle axe said.

"Yes, Stepmother." Vi adjusted the cloche hat in the mirror and nodded to the dress shop girl, adding several pairs of stockings to her pile.

Lady Eleanor's gaze sharpened on the stockings but she didn't say a word. They'd already discussed her dress choices and her inexplicable demand for an education wherein she hadn't bothered to find a young man from a good family.

"I would think after all this time you could remember to call me mother. You know how your father feels about it."

"Of course," Violet said, refusing to use the word.

Stepmother sniffed and then said, "You and Victor are going to Agatha's for Christmas?"

"Yes, ma'am." Violet nodded to the kid gloves, and the shop girl winked and slid them into the pile without her stepmother even taking note.

"She has a lot of money, Violet. Make yourself useful to her. Victor barely has enough to live on as it is. If he wants to marry, he'll need you gone and something more."

Violet didn't bother rehashing that their father had rather enough money for both Violet and Victor. They each had inherited money from their grandfather, their mother, and had an allowance from their father. Victor would, however, get more money when he turned twenty-five and Violet would receive something when she married. Neither of them were hard-up, so the melodramatics about Violet becoming an old maid had another purpose.

Violet smiled winningly at the shop girl and turned to examine Lady Eleanor. She was a lovely creature.

"Look, Violet," Stepmother said, "I am trying to do my best by you. You know that. Isolde is going off to university, and she's going because she wants to meet a good young man. Surely you don't think that you'll ever marry if Isolde beats you to the altar? My dear, she is *five* years younger than you."

Violet could feel a pulsing at her temples that didn't ease with the pile of lovely things.

"Violet? I am talking to you."

The shop girl winced and then placed an embroidered silk scarf on the pile for Violet along with another pair of stockings. Her step-mother didn't even notice. Violet tapped the counter where a very long strand of jet beads was artfully laid out.

"It is possible given Isolde's wants as compared to my own," Violet said, drawing attention to herself while the shop girl put the beads on Violet's pile of things, "That she might marry before myself. That is the desire of her heart, not mine."

"It should concern you," Stepmother hissed. "You will be *on the shelf.* You'll have to *work* to support yourself when Victor gives up supporting you. He will, Violet."

"Victor?" Vi asked.

Lady Eleanor trod over Violet's insertion and said, "He will marry and he will need to take care *of his wife!*"

Violet sniffed once and said to the shop girl, "I think we've got all we need. Thank you for your help. You can send the bill to Carlyle house and the items to the address I gave you."

Violet turned to her stepmother and tried to avoid an utter breach. "Lady Eleanor, thank you for caring."

"Of course I care," she said, nodding in agreement of Violet's instructions. "I'm *trying* to do what's best for you."

"You are," Violet agreed gently. "It's just that it's not your day any longer, and I am not you or Isolde. I am not going to marry whichever semi-decent man you throw in my path."

"Then what *will* you do?"

"I suppose, if it comes to it, I'll work." Violet enjoyed her step-mother's wince too much.

"Work?" Lady Eleanor pressed her hand to her chest and backed away.

"I will not be the first woman who chooses to support herself rather than marry someone I don't care for. Not even if that man is rolling in the green."

"Working isn't a game, Violet! You are spoilt! And that is your problem. These modern young things who think they know better than their elders. There is quite a lot to be said for a comfortable home and a man who puts you above all others. Whatever will you do to work?"

"I don't know," Violet admitted. "Lila writes magazine articles. Perhaps something like that. I could be a typist, I suppose. I have a friend who takes photographs. I'm sure I can come up with something."

"Your father will be hearing of this," Lady Eleanor hissed, sweeping from the shop.

Violet turned to the shop girl. "I think this means that I need to add that shawl there. And perhaps a few more pairs of stockings. They do go so quickly."

"She's awful," the girl said and then blushed, glancing behind her to ensure no one else had heard.

"Mmmm," Violet said, raising her brows in agreement. Lady Eleanor wasn't quite the worst. She wanted things her way, certainly. As much as Violet despised that, Eleanor also wanted Violet safe and cared for.

"Maybe you could design dresses. There's a squire's daughter who does that," the girl said. She brought Violet over to a champagne pink gown and said, "She made this. She sells through our shop and another in Paris."

Violet ooohed and checked the watch pinned her jacket and then said, "I think I've got time to try that beauty on."

"Will you really get a job?" the girl asked.

Vi supposed the idea of being able to afford to live without working was ridiculous to someone in a shop.

She shrugged and then admitted, "If I wanted to stay in London and Vic really did throw me out. Only my brother would never, ever do that. Besides, he's barely twenty-three. I might be old to get married, but he's too young."

CHAPTER TWO

"*H*ullo, hullo, hullo, Vi darling, is that you?"

Violet spun around with a grin on her face and tucked a few strands of hair behind her ear. Her gaze fixed upon the bright cheeks and perfectly shingled hair and they both squealed like school girls.

"Gwennie!"

They rushed each other like the chums they were and didn't quite kiss. Carefully applied lipstick could be smudged so easily.

"Gwennie! Whatever are you doing here? Weren't you bouncing around Scotland with your mum?"

She shook her head and her blonde hair flew with the movement. Her bright brown eyes flashed with irritation and her nose crinkled as she said, "My aunt Gertie! It was awful. She's a stern old thing and I spent rather too much time embroidering seat cushions."

Vi winced and squeezed Gwennie's hand before tucking it into the crook of her arm and said, "But you're here now? You've escaped!"

"Thank goodness. Good old Lila and Denny offered to let me come and stay with them for a while when they heard I was ready to throw myself from the highest tower to find an inch of freedom. So I legged it and here I am!"

"And your aunt..." Vi trailed off. She might not have seen Gwennie in simply ages, but she remembered the tune. Gwennie's Aunt Gertrude held the purse strings for Gwennie and did not believe in modern girls. She objected to dancing, drinking, playing cards, and anything that wasn't entirely Victorian.

"Well," Gwennie said in an aside, "She doesn't *love* that I'm here. But Lila is from *such a good family*. And, of course, she and Denny are married. So, Gertie thinks that they'll throw me in the way of dashing and well-connected lads. Perhaps with a touch of a fortune."

Vi winced. Gertrude couldn't be more wrong about Lila and Denny. Most of their friends were starving artists or people Gwennie already knew.

Gwennie raised her brows and said, "She thinks Denny's friends must be matrimonially inclined since he was."

Vi choked at that. Matrimonially inclined? Denny's friends? She laughed. He and Lila had been besotted since they were in the nursery. Their marriage was as fated as the rising sun and they hadn't seen the need to wait.

As far as marriage went, Vi had been hearing that same horrid tune from her stepmother, Lady Eleanor. Thankfully, with Victor's support and her own small inheritance, Vi wasn't quite at daggers drawn with her stepmother. It was getting awfully near to hand as she got older. If Vi went to one more family dinner with some eligible cove sitting by ready to consider her, she might go stark raving mad. It was as though they appeared assuming she was theirs for the taking and all they needed to do was decide whether she'd do. No one seemed to think she deserved to be anything other than grateful.

"Whatever are you doing for tea, darling?" Vi asked, "Would you like to nip home for a bit of something with Vic and I? Vic has found the most wonderful man to help us; I'm sure it'll be scrumptious. Shall we ring up Lila and Denny and bring them along?"

"Oh, that does sound lovely. To get the old girls together. Do you ever miss the school days?"

"Never," Vi admitted. "I was grateful to Aunt Agatha for letting me go to college. You know my father and stepmother expected me to meet someone and marry. Dear Aunt Agatha wanted me to be educated. Not wanted. Expected. You know, the old girl made me write to her about what I was learning and whatnot. Vic and I both, since she paid for him too."

Gwennie laughed and then said, "I wish my aunt was a bit more like yours."

"Well, Aggie was something of a firebrand in her day. Still is, come to think of it."

~

"What's all this then?" Vic asked as he came into the drawing room where they were lounging with their tea.

"Hullo, Vic!" Vi called. "You remember Lila and Denny and of course, Gwennie."

He glanced around the room, nodded, and simply slid into one of the sitting chairs.

"Vic! Whatever is the matter?" Vi asked as she poured him a stiff coffee, bypassing the tea she knew he didn't want and making him a plate of biscuits and cake.

"I can't eat darling," he said. "It's too, too bad. We shall need to leave at once. Well..."

"At once? But we have dinner plans and our friends are here."

He groaned and then said, "Well, not at once. In the morning, it's Aggie. The old bean has demanded we appear early. For an *extended* house party with the relatives."

"What?" The twins had planned to head to their aunt's home for Christmas, but that wasn't for a fortnight. Perhaps a long weekend. Maybe a few days longer if the rest of the relatives fled quickly. "No."

"Indeed. She sounded rather weak and washy, too. Simply threw herself upon us to come and rescue her."

"She couldn't have," Vi said.

"She did, I tell you. She did. I read the letter and it was as clear as day."

"But...I don't want to go for a fortnight plus the hols," Vic said, shoving his plate of biscuits back into his lap. She knew him rather well, and when he was hungry he was a bit of a wilting flower. She shook her head at him and headed back across the room to her seat.

well, and when he was hungry he was a bit of a wilting flower. She shook her head at him and headed back across the room to her seat.

"It's worse than you know," he moaned, shoving a whole biscuit into his mouth and talking around it. "She's invited everyone. And she sent a telegraph as well. It came after you left."

Vi blinked, turning slowly back to her brother, shaking her head.

"Indeed. She has. All of them."

"But..."

"Yes," he said, flatly draining his coffee and then rubbing his stomach as though he shouldn't have.

"No."

"It's true," he said weakly. "I saw Algernon at the club when the telegraph arrived. He's got one too, and he's bringing a friend. Possibly two."

"Oh no," Vi said as she dropped into her seat. "Not..."

"Theodophilus? Yes."

Vi shivered. Their cousin Algernon was a blighter. But his friends were worse. Somehow Algernon gave them the impression that he was close to Vi and Vic and that she was up for grabs. Everyone knew that her father would settle a lump of green on her when she married. Algernon seemed to think it was his to half-offer her and the money to his friends.

"I won't do it," Vi said flatly.

"It's Aggie."

Vi bit her lip, glancing at her friends who were watching the exchange with hawk eyes.

"Did you say that Algie is bringing a friend or two?"

"Yes, darling. Asking again won't change things."

"Then we will too." Vi looked at her friends and said, "You're conscripted."

"Oh, but..."

"Rally round, darlings. We need you." She tapped her cheek and then the most enchanting thought occurred to her. "On the way back, we'll swing through Paris and have a lovely time for a few days. Isn't Tomas in Paris? Didn't he say he rented that big house, Vic?"

"Tomas is in love with you, Vi."

"Then he won't object to our arrival."

"Rather mercenary of you, luv," Vic said. "We'll need something to look forward to if we have to spend so long with Algie and the other blood-suckers."

"Mmmm." Vi turned her gaze to her friends. "Please? Please darlings? It won't be all bad. There's a pond for skating and Aggie isn't cheap when it comes to the vittles. She's a mouthy old thing and can be trusted to not control our every move. We could dance some, listen to music, see a bit of the countryside if the weather isn't too bad."

"Denny can you take that much time off?"

"Ah..."

"Paris. Booze. Skating?" Vi wheedled, glancing at Lila who turned her big eyes on her love with a pleading look.

He hemmed and hawed before he said, "I really only half-work anyway. Just enough to keep the pater happy that I'm doing something and keep my allowance coming."

"Then it's resolved! Motion carried. All for one and one for all," Vi laughed.

"This calls for drinks," Victor said, but Vi scowled at him and waved hers away. She had a firm policy of never drinking while she was still struggling with the headache from the last round.

Giles came into the sitting room with another tray of sandwiches and said, "Your new things have arrived, miss."

"Lovely," Vi said. "Come, darlings, and see what I earned this morning."

"What did Eleanor say about me?" Vic asked rather anxiously as Vi rose.

"That your eventual wife would throw me out and I'd have to marry or slum it."

Vic laughed at that and Vi led the girls to her room where Lila threw herself on the bed and Gwennie started to dig through the bags that had arrived.

"You simply robbed her blind, Vi," Gwennie said, as she pulled out the stack of stockings.

"It's not quite so simple as that. Father won't give me an allowance without strings, but he'll still pay for clothes," Vi said. "I just bought rather more than Eleanor realized. Father won't object when he gets the bill. He doesn't get all that many bills from me. I always look like the economical sister because Isolde goes ham."

"Oh, that *is* nice," Gwennie said. "I wish my parents or aunt would do the same. Rather than letting me buy clothes, they simply buy a dress they approve of here or there. Or gift me with a new hat. I get stockings money and not enough for much more. I have to beg for cigarettes."

"Money is the string they use to get us to do what they want us to do," Lila said, "It doesn't get better after you are married. Denny and I get quiet little questions about babies. My mother can't imagine that I might be doing anything to prevent a baby and I don't think Father is even aware that such things exist. They're both quite concerned that I'm barren and Denny will leave me."

"There's time left for babies," Gwennie said, holding up the pink champagne dress against herself. "This is divine."

"It is," Vi agreed. "Thank you for coming with us. The relatives really are rather vile. Aunt Agatha is a doll. An armed and slightly mad doll, but a doll all the same. And you never know who will be with Aunt Agatha. Anything from a painter Lady Eleanor would find objectionable to some rich duke's son."

"That sounds interesting," Lila admitted. "Better than withering away at home while Denny pretends to work."

"It sounds about a million times better than slowly dying with my aunt in Scotland."

"Darlings," Vi said, rising smoothly and adjusting her cuffs. "I'm without a maid, so I'll be having to pack while we chat since Harold Lannister has tickets for *So This is London* and I very much want to go."

"You're wearing this, I hope," Gwennie said, nudging the dress.

Vi smirked and nodded, holding the dress against her body and twirling so it flew out. "Why else would I buy it?"

"Is Harold Lannister rich?" Lila demanded.

"Is he handsome?" Gwennie touched the dress almost longingly.

"He's—witty. Educated. Not ugly, but not handsome. And very, very rich."

"Is he connected to the right families?" Lila asked, channeling Lady Eleanor.

"He's American," Vi said with a wicked grin. "Lady Eleanor would despise him."

CHAPTER THREE

"Solve a puzzle for me, darling?" Lila asked as the group settled into their seats in the train carriage.

Vi glanced her way and said, "Well of course. If you need brain-work, I'm the one."

"Why are we going to this thing? Aunt Agatha is not like Gwennie's aunt who pays for things, right?"

"You mean she doesn't give us an allowance?" Victor asked. He smiled at Vi and then turned back to Lila and Denny.

"Correct," Lila said. "I understood when you wrote to her weekly about what you were learning at school. She paid the bills then."

Vi laughed. "It's rather simple. We like her."

"Love her even," Victor added, tapping his cigarette case against his thigh. Violet had given him it as a reward for crawling out of college, degree clutched in his paw.

"But you're not her heir?" Denny asked. "She's rather rolling in the green, isn't she?"

"Funny you should ask," Victor said. "I am the keeper of the bet book on that. Vi hasn't placed a bet, but the rest of us have quite a sum on the line."

"That bet book is foul." Violet glanced across the aisle and found a rather distinguished older man sitting next to a younger version of himself. The older man had glanced their way when they were talking of the bet book and she was sure he was listening.

"It is foul," Victor agreed blithely. "Without taste and generally despicable."

"Stop quoting me," she said, elbowing him. She tried to direct his attention to their eavesdropper but Denny snatched the book from Vic's hand. It was a small black thing, and it held more of Vic's despicable side than she wanted to know.

"Let's see," Denny said, flipping the pages and opening one at random. "Oh ho, it's the Algernon page. He thinks Violet and Victor will inherit. With rather too much for the servants. And not a penny to those who need it. He's rather an obnoxious fathead, isn't he?"

Vi nodded and adjusted her coat. "Oh, stop."

Denny grinned at her and turned another page. "Ah, cousin Meredith. Her guess was probably a house of wayward girls. Is she a sour one?"

"Not awfully," Vi said, "She's just on the border of things. Not rich but not poor. She's too close to the big houses and the fancy parties to be satisfied with what she has. Only she's too far away to be able to really slide in and enjoy."

"I know the type," Denny said blithely. He had already lit his cigarette and took a long drag.

"If dear cousin Meredith had the looks, she'd weasel her way into some rich man's bed and find it wasn't all she thought," Vic said

"Victor Carlyle," Vi countered. "There is nothing wrong with Meredith."

"I like Merry," Vic said while Lila laughed. "One has to be rather *the thing* to marry for money. She's lovely enough but in a rather ordinary way. Not like Lila. Even you couldn't do it, Vi. Not on looks. Whoever gets you will be obsessed with your wit and then never think anyone else could rival you."

"Stop it," Vi said, elbowing her brother rather harder this time. "You know I don't wish to marry for money."

"If you did, you'd marry Tomas who has enough money to bathe in and worships the ground you walk on."

Vi had had enough of that. "I'm going to find wherever Gwennie disappeared to."

"You know she gets sick on trains," Lila called, "You may not want to find her."

"She's not the only one ready to sick up." Vi shook her head, walking away.

As she left she heard Denny ask, "And who does Vi think your aunt will leave her money to?"

"Vi? She refuses to say. She really does hate this thing. It only exists because of one drunken evening, but even in her cups, she wouldn't bet. It's anyone's guess who will inherit and no one would be surprised if she left it all to one of us, split it evenly, or decided to fund a reform school for girls," Vic said. "Drives most of the family mad."

"A reform school for girls," Denny squeaked. "No wonder! Why does Algie think it'll be you? The poor fish. You all have never given the idea that it would be."

Victor hummed and then said, "Oh our mother asked Aunt Agatha to look after us when Mum realized she was dying. Dear old Aggie took her promise seriously. Trying to compel us to read treatises and learn about investments. Vi always indulged the old dear. I'm afraid I never did. But, she also saw that we learned to ride and paid for our tour around the world. She's a good 'un, and Vi doesn't want to think about her dying."

"So Agatha is a bit more of a replacement mother than Lady Eleanor," Denny mused.

"Clearly, darling," Lila told her husband. "Don't be thick."

Violet Carlyle looked up from adjusting her fur-trimmed coat to see her cousin Meredith's pale face. Her nose was powdered, her hair was tucked up into an updo that gave the illusion of a bob, and her cheeks were as bright as her eyes. Violet almost felt drab in comparison. Her own dark hair was held against her head with a rather delightful hat, and she knew the dark color brought out the brightness of her eyes. She might have more freckles than she could hide, and she might be curvier than was the fashion, but she knew she was cute as a button. Meredith, however, was elegant and slim.

"Meredith, luv," Violet said, pressing her cheek against her cousin's. "How long has it been? Ages? Simply ages!"

"Oh, simply forever. Is Victor with you?"

"Of course." Vi grinned. "He's in the carriage smoking and drinking coffee with a few friends. Are you coming down alone? How modern of you!"

Vi let her gaze flit over her cousin, noting her threadbare, too-thin coat and slightly dented cloche. Vi felt a bit like a poisonous piece of work when she realized how hard-up Meredith seemed. Vi knew in a relatively distant way that Meredith had married and lost her husband during the war, but Vi hadn't understood that her cousin had fallen onto such hard times.

"I wasn't expecting you'd be on the same train," Vi said, not letting her gaze linger on anything other than her cousin's face. "Isn't it lovely? Victor wired for a car to be waiting for us and for someone to take our luggage. You'll join us, won't you dear?"

Meredith accepted and then complained about the drizzle outside before stating, "This is my first holiday with Aunt Agatha in quite some time. Have you been down recently?"

"Victor and I tend to spend Christmas more with Aunt Agatha than our father. She's such a grand gal and Papa is never quite pleased with Victor or myself, don't you know."

Meredith's face froze for a moment and Vi was sure she knew why. Meredith hoped to inherit from Aunt Agatha. It drove Violet mad that whenever any of Agatha's relatives saw her they seemed to only see money bags up for the taking. What about her adventures? What about how she'd married, lost her husband, and spent the next forty years investing and growing his respectable income into something rather remarkable. As a woman!

"Oh, Vi," Gwennie said from behind them. "I wonder if you wouldn't hunt me up some water, dear?"

"Oh, you poor thing," Violet said, "You look simply deathly. Come, come. Can I get you anything else?"

"Oh no...no..." She heaved some and came all over green. Violet backed up a step in case it was a projectile situation.

Meredith wrapped an arm around Gwennie's shoulders and walked her to an empty seat, placing the bucket from a ready porter into Gwennie's lap while Violet disappeared to find a cup of water. And perhaps a fortifying cup of tea?

Violet rushed down the train aisle looking for a porter or a tea cart to gather up the necessaries for Gwennie and crashed right into the strapping man who had been sitting across the aisle from her and her friends.

"Oh! Oh, I'm so sorry. So clumsy of me. I'm afraid I..."

He cut in with a low manly voice that caught her attention. "Don't think a thing of it. I was right in your path."

"And I barged right into you," she said and smiled. Rather nervously, she adjusted her hat. He was so tall. And dashing. With a rather severe jaw and penetrating eyes. He had one of those beefy, strong bodies that made her feel tiny, which wasn't something she knew she liked until quite this moment. Given her luck, the most probable outcome was that he was a dunce.

"Brightest part of my day," he said, and he stole another smile from her without her consent.

She took a look about the compartment and caught the positively judgmental gaze of Meredith. Violet flinched. "Oh, excuse me. I must get my friend some water. Please forgive me for simply slamming into you." She nodded and flowed down the aisle hoping to improve the impression he must have of her. 'Oh Violet,' she thought, 'It is not like you'll see him again.'

She gathered up both a cup of tea and a glass of water for poor Gwennie and made her way back to where she'd left the girls only to find them gone. By Jove, whatever was Meredith thinking taking Gwennie off when Violet was out getting the necessaries? Violet scrunched up her nose, shrugged her shoulders, and decided the best course was to head back to her brother and see if Gwennie had turned up there.

The train carriage where her brother and friends were sitting did, in fact, contain Meredith and a green Gwennie. Vi delivered the now barely warm cuppa and the water and hoped to not wear it should it return to existence.

The gentleman she'd abused in the aisle hadn't returned, but the man who simply must be his father remained. Meredith had taken an empty seat down the way and Vi let her hand touch Victor's shoulder before she made her way down to their cousin.

"How have you been, Meredith?" Violet asked, in a jolly tone.

"As well as can be expected," Meredith replied, rather poisonously.

Violet pasted a bright smile over her face and commented upon the newly dropped waistlines.

"I don't waste my time, energy, or money with such frivolities. Very few have the time or money to fritter away like you and Victor."

Violet was simply determined to not let Meredith spread her blighted outlook, so she smiled and said, "We *have* been rather blessed, haven't we? Funny how the luxury of our *shared* grandfather and the little bit of money from our mother has given us such the chance for—how did you say it? A frivolous life."

Something seemed to whisper judgement and sour lemons to her cousin and Meredith's mouth twisted up into a bit of a snarl. She snuffled a little bit and then said in a rather boiled way, "Yes. Well. I suppose we did receive a similar inheritance from our grandfather. Of course your father has added a bit to yours. And you didn't have the burden of marriage, a household, and then losing your beloved in the war."

A great tear rolled down Meredith's face, and Violet was suddenly convicted of being the sour one. She reached forward and took Meredith's hand. "You have had a time of it, haven't you? Oh, darling. I suppose I am just unable to understand the greatness of your loss."

Meredith pulled out a worn handkerchief, and Violet felt another flash of guilt. Her poor cousin. Even her handkerchiefs looked as if they'd been through the war. And perhaps they had.

"I can only hope that Aunt Agatha will understand. You would think that a widow, like herself, would be able to see why I struggle so."

The inference to Aunt Agatha's will was a bit too blunt for Violet's taste. The last thing she wanted was to keep her eye on Aunt Agatha's death as something to be anticipated. Perhaps she was being too harsh on Meredith? She might merely intend to put the touch on Aunt Agatha for a bit of green. Neither was to Violet's taste, but one intention was infinitely preferable.

CHAPTER FOUR

*T*he drive from the train station to Aunt Agatha's countryside
manor was longer than poor Gwennie could handle and they
had to pull over for her to sick up and then for Denny to sympathetically sick up alongside her.

Violet fled the area while the two of them were clearing their stomachs on the road. Otherwise, she just might have joined the lineup of
the ill. Lila and Victor, who had rather stronger stomachs than Violet,
attended the downtrodden while Meredith remained in the car.

"Miss," the driver said, "There is a car coming if I don't mishear.
Perhaps a step to the side of the road?"

"Thank you, Peters." Violet selected the side of the road without
people sicking up and turned her face up to the drizzle. "Am I mad to
enjoy the smell of the rain in the countryside?"

"Perhaps a little, miss," he said kindly. His craggy face spread with a
grin and a wink and he said, "But then again country rain is better than
that dirty London rain."

"Too right you are, Peters," Vi said.

A few moments later a Rolls-Royce Silver Ghost paused beside the
road. The driver's door opened and the glorious man from the train
stepped out.

"Oh hello," Violet said, smiling at him. "If it isn't my train friend, the punching bag."

"You are rather too small to do much damage. Don't worry too much."

He grinned at her. His companion, the suspected father, stepped out of the other side of the car. "Is all well here, my dear?"

"Well," Violet said, "Our automobile is well and the journey proceeds afoot with but a small hiccup."

They turned and saw the sick Gwennie and Denny. A smile flitted across the face of the son who said, "And you are no nursemaid?"

"Alas," Violet laughed, "We've already got one who is sympathetically ill and I have no desire to add to that number."

"Wise, wise," the older man said. "I believe you are Violet Carlyle."

Violet placed her hand on her chest, a little surprised, and said, "I am, indeed. You, I fear, have the better of me."

"Not for long," he said, "I am James Wakefield and this is my son, Jack."

"Misters Wakefield," Violet said, waiting for the rest of the explanation.

"My father is great chums with your aunt," the younger Mr. Wakefield said. "We are to be part of this holiday party."

"Oh, hullo," Violet said, holding out her hand to each of them in turn. "That does explain it. Victor and I had heard dear Aunt Agatha had invited most of the family and rather expected her interesting friends as well."

"I don't know about interesting," the older Mr. Wakefield said. "Lady Agatha's husband and I were school chums through Eton and Oxford. Her invitation forced my poor son to listen to too many tales about the good old days."

"I'm sure he enjoyed every minute of it," she laughed. Victor joined Violet and she introduced her twin to her aunt's guests. They were a bit stiffer with her brother and Violet was suddenly sure they'd heard the discussion of the betting book. Oh, her brother was a dunce! She wanted to take him aside and lecture him about his poor taste again but knew it would do no good.

A rather contemplative silence crossed the group and Victor said,

"Well luv, we should probably get back on the road and hope that poor Gwennie can make it the rest of the way. I imagine crossing the channel will be even more exciting for our little group."

"It was a pleasure, my dear," the older Mr. Wakefield said, with a boiled glance at Victor. The younger Mr. Wakefield took Vi's hand and squeezed it. She admitted, if only privately, that her attention was well and truly caught. She pushed the thought aside by imagining the victorious crowing of her stepmother should Violet succumb to these softer feelings.

"Gentlemen," she said brightly, as they stepped back into their car, waiting for her companions to get their car out of the road and on with their journey.

"That old guy is a rather phlegmatic old bird, isn't he?" Victor said as they joined their friends.

"Victor! They heard your conversation about betting on Aunt Agatha's will."

He cast her a green glance and then said, "Oh. Well. Oh dear. You don't think…"

"That he'll tell Aunt Agatha? I simply have no idea, my dear. But I did tell you."

"There it is. That blighted and deserved, 'I told you so.' How you love to tell me, 'I told you so.' It is a good thing I adore you, sister mine."

"What's this now?" Meredith queried imperiously.

Violet disguised a sigh with a yawn and said, "Victor's humor is sometimes in rather poor taste."

"Well! He is a man," Meredith almost snarled.

Violet cracked the window to disperse the remaining smell of sick that lingered on. Perhaps someone had it on their shoes? She really must be sure to tip Peters particularly well since he'd be cleaning this mess out.

The long drive up to Aunt Agatha's house was lined with oak trees that spread naked branches over the lane. Those ended with a parade of hedges clipped into whimsical animal shapes. Then the drive circled around a large fountain that housed a Greek statue some distant relative had acquired from ancient ruins.

"Who is the statue?" Gwennie breathed. "Oh, this house. It's just lovely."

"Another of the family bets," Vic said blithely. "Violet says it's Nyx. Everyone else says it's a random Greek woman. But I find Violet to be invariably right."

Violet grinned at Victor who knew all too well she'd stated Nyx, using authority in her tone, only to make their cousin Algernon second-guess himself. She winked at Victor and then saw Algernon and Theodophilus's faces in the window of one of the front rooms.

"Oh look." Vic glanced at the others and then jerked his head towards the window. "The reasons we needed to rally the troops."

"Reporting for duty, Captain." Lila leaned forward to push Denny's hair back. He still looked as though he'd jogged through a jungle and was green to boot. "I'll need a sidecar to see me through."

"Or two," Denny added. "With a gin rickey chaser."

"Aunt Agatha always has a well-stocked bar, and Giles is bringing some of my own collection as well. We'll have options, dear ones," Victor said, eyeing Gwennie's heaving with concern.

"You won't be drinking anything, my lad," Lila told Denny, "Until you've returned to your normal ruddy self."

The Wakefield car pulled up behind them as Peters handed Violet out of the car. The Wakefields' driver opened the door for their car and they were joined on the steps up to the house.

Agatha's butler opened the door as they approached and Violet said, "Oh, Hargreaves! Suddenly all is well in the world. How *are* you?"

"Delighted to see you, miss. Mrs. Davies is waiting in the violet room. She said to feel free to freshen up before you come down. There's tea and sandwiches when you're ready. If you'd rather, we'll send some up to you."

"Oh, you are simply the best, Hargreaves!" Violet said and glanced at Victor, who took her hand and led them inside.

They were followed by their friends and led off to their bedrooms. Aunt Agatha was in the east wing and Violet and her friends were led to the west wing. Violet had the room she always used, with Meredith down the hall and Gwennie next door. Lila and Denny shared a room across the hall and Victor was directly across from Violet as per usual.

Violet saw her friends to their rooms and disappeared. Poor Gwennie—and probably Denny—needed to rest up a bit and maybe eat some dry toast. Violet requested the offered tea to their rooms so that her friends could recover, and the maid, Hargreaves's niece Beatrice, nodded and darted off. She was a sprightly thing for a housemaid.

"Did you see that the Wakefield gentlemen were taken directly to Agatha?" Victor asked as Violet opened her bedroom door. "Odd that. Seems like she'd have them freshen up, but I heard Hargreaves tell the gents Aggie wanted to see them right away."

"That is odd," Violet said. "Perhaps they're better friends than we knew."

"Surely we'd have heard of him after all this time?"

Violet wasn't so sure of that. Aunt Agatha had many friends through her business dealings. When you added in the artists she patronized and the family connections, Agatha was rarely alone in her home.

"Even still," Victor mused, "It isn't like dear Aggie to not let her friends get comfortable."

"She's been acting odd, really. It's not like her to push the other relatives into Christmas. How long has it been since we've seen Meredith? Since her husband died? And yet...she's here. Along with us and Algernon and who knows else. Something is up, my lad."

Victor and Violet met gazes and he shrugged. A rush of worry crossed through Violet and she wondered why the Wakefields? The man and his son seemed an odd addition to a family party. Maybe Violet would be less concerned if she'd met them before, but she and Victor had come to Christmas with Aunt Agatha since they'd turned five years old, and Violet was certain she'd never heard the name Wakefield before.

CHAPTER FIVE

"*I*s it true, my dear?" Aunt Agatha asked as Violet entered the violet room after she'd brushed her hair, freshened her makeup, and changed out of her traveling clothes.

"Is what true, dear aunt?" Violet crossed to her aunt and kissed each cheek before saying, "You look smashing, darling."

"Don't lie to me, brat. I know I look awful. I haven't been sleeping well and it shows. Is it true that you turned down Tomas St. Mark's invitation to marriage?"

Violet leaned away from her aunt, still keeping Agatha's hands in her own and then nodded. Violet squeezed Agatha's hands once again, let them, go, and dropped into an arm chair near the fire. "Seeing you is always a joy, my love. Even if you aren't feeling quite the thing. As for Tomas, I don't love him like he deserves."

"He's very rich," Aunt Agatha said with a raised brow. There was something in that statement that didn't sound quite like Agatha. That was something Lady Eleanor would say, not Aunt Agatha. Lady Eleanor had expected Violet to marry for connections and money. Aunt Agatha had taught Violet to manage her own money and saw to her education, so she could work if she chose.

"Darling," Violet sighed, "I need a drink if we're going to be discussing my status as a pauper and why I should marry for money."

Violet crossed to the drink cart and made herself a sidecar and another for Aunt Agatha. Violet handed the drink to her aunt and then slid back into the seat by the fire.

"Yes, Tomas is simply swimming in cash. Not just as compared to myself but as compared to most of the human race. The thing that drives me utterly up the wall is that I can be quite comfortable with the money Mama left me. Why should I sell myself? For what? A pretty car? A mansion? Jewels? Surely happiness is worth more than a castle in the back of beyond. Besides, I love Tomas. I just don't *love* him, and I couldn't promise to be his, knowing I could never give him what he really wants."

Aunt Agatha raised a brow at Violet, who huffed before adding, "Not that. My heart. He wants me to love him above all. Maybe in time I would love him that way, but what if I didn't? I can't promise to fall in love with him."

Aunt Agatha sipped the sidecar, shuddered, and set it aside.

Violet laughed at the look on her aunt's face and then added, "I won't trap him, be unable to give him the love he wants, and then see him broken further by me. I won't do it."

Aunt Agatha leaned back, crossing her fingers over her stomach before she asked, archly, "And how does Lady Eleanor feel about your decision?"

"Don't be daft, dear Aggie. I haven't told her about the offer. It is, unfortunately, a standing offer. If Eleanor knew...well...she and Papa might lock me in my room and beat me until I said yes or something else as Victorian."

"I'm concerned you'd be right about that. Your father...." Aunt Agatha cut off her statement and then said, "Well...we have our differences. Tell me, has Victor decided to get a job?"

Violet flinched for her brother. She paused and then said, "Victor doesn't need the money either. At least not while he isn't supporting a wife and children."

"Does he still feel guilty for living?"

Violet sighed and nodded. Victor had been called up to duty in the war. In training, his shoulder had been broken. By the time he was healed, the men Victor would have served with were dead in the trenches and the war was over. Survivor's guilt colored his thoughts whenever he allowed himself to think too much about it. It didn't seem to matter that he'd shown up for duty and done his best. No one blamed him except himself, but he couldn't quite shake it. Tomas had been with Victor and he'd ended in the trenches. He carried scars and waking nightmares from a few short months.

Victor had loved those men who had died. They'd been brothers in their hearts. An accident of fate had saved Victor. Violet wouldn't deny she was grateful her twin had survived. Of her four brothers, she only had two left. Their eldest brother had been the heir to the earldom. He'd served, but in an office where there was little threat to his life.

Their brother Peter had died weeks into his service when his plane had gone down. Their brother Lionel had contracted the Spanish Flu in the trenches and never come home. There wasn't a day that went by where Violet wasn't just grateful that Victor had made it through.

Agatha ignored the burden of the war for Victor—they all knew he'd been lucky. "He needs to build a career now if he wants to support the woman he loves later."

Violet didn't argue with Agatha but she didn't agree either. Victor was an adult. He'd heard all the arguments, and they had their secret project, their investments, and they were more frugal than one might expect of them.

Violet drained her drink and debated getting well and truly into her cups, but she couldn't do that to her aunt. "Tell me what's wrong, Aunt. Why aren't you sleeping?"

Aunt Agatha examined Violet's face as if searching for something and then said, "Someone is trying to kill me."

Violet choked and leaned forward, coughing. The door opened while Violet was hacking into her handkerchief. Meredith, Algernon, and that fiend, Theodophilus, entered the room as Violet recovered. Where were her friends? They were supposed to rally round. She needed them to distract the others, so Violet could delve into Aunt Agatha's horrifying statement.

Aunt Agatha shot Violet a look when she could breathe again that was an obvious order to keep her trap shut.

Theodophilus crossed to Violet with a glass of seltzer water as she stopped coughing. Violet took it, but she wanted to toss it in his face when she noted his eyes on her chest.

"Would you care for a walk before dinner, Violet?"

Violet smiled charmingly and said, "I've brought friends, Mr. Smythe-Hill. I can hardly leave them just as we arrive. Thank you for the invitation."

She rose and stepped closer to Agatha. Standing had been to keep him from looming over her, but now that she had, she felt as though she'd just put herself on display for him. Theodophilus smirked at Violet, letting his eyes drift down her body, and she shot him a nasty look. He just grinned though, as if she were playing with him instead of disgusted by his attention.

They'd met far too often in London and she'd done all she could to dissuade his attention from her. He seemed to think she was avoiding him to entice him instead of just disinterested.

"Well, my dear, are you well now?" Aunt Agatha gave Theodophilus her own nasty look and he cleared his throat, excused himself, and stepped across the room to accept a drink from Victor, who was playing bartender.

Victor's man Giles must have arrived with Victor's stash of his own booze because Violet noticed the tell-tale signs of a grasshopper being mixed.

"What's all this about, Aunt?" Algernon demanded as he crossed to them, cocktail in hand. He sounded aggrieved as though he had been attacked. "Why did you need us all here?"

Violet glanced around thinking about Aunt Agatha's statement. She hadn't been sleeping; she thought someone might be trying to kill her. *Why?* What had happened? As Violet examined the guests, she realized most of Agatha's possible heirs were present. Violet shuddered as she glanced around the room. If someone was trying to kill Aunt Agatha, the likeliest motive was money, seeing as how she was notoriously swimming in the green.

She must see them all as suspects. Violet felt a flash of hurt as she realized she was included in that number. Didn't Aunt Agatha know that Violet would never hurt her? Agatha was a near mother to Violet and Victor. Who had they turned to time and again? Aunt Agatha. Just the thought of losing her made Violet's heart stutter.

Violet looked around the room again. Everyone had put on their shiny clothes and brushed their shoes. They were all pretending to be happy to be together, but they weren't. Not really. Violet would never had spent Christmas with Algernon and his friend. Violet might have been happy to have lunch with Meredith, but Merry wouldn't have been Violet's first choice for the hols.

Her gaze crossed the room again, noting each person. Victor—both suspect and twin. But Violet would swear on her dying breath that Victor would never hurt anyone, let alone their aunt. Denny, Lila, and Gwennie were only here because Violet and Victor had invited them, and they'd never be real suspects of course.

There was a tall man in a pinstriped suit with slicked back red hair and a slew of freckles over his nose. He reminded Violet of someone, but she couldn't quite place him. She sighed and looked beyond him to that blighter, Algernon.

They were all cousins. Aunt Agatha was their great aunt. She'd never had children of her own, but her brother had Kingsley, Cecil, and the twins' mother, Penelope.

Cousin Algernon was the oldest child of Kingsley. As children, the twins had seen Algernon quite often. He had two more siblings, but they were quite a bit younger and hadn't been half-raised by Aunt Agatha.

Meredith's father, Uncle Cecil, had quite a falling out with Aunt Agatha years ago. He'd been told once, in no uncertain terms, that he was a nasty piece of work and he would have no more chance at an inheritance from Agatha than he would from the queen. His response had been to throw Meredith at Aunt Agatha and not bother to go along on visits himself.

It was family legend that Meredith had been chosen because he figured she was the least marriageable of his daughters. Cecil had hoped Meredith might get the money from his aunt that he'd lost. Violet winced at the memory, almost certain it was true. Meredith's sister Gertrude had never shown up at those summers with Aunt Agatha.

Instead, poor Meredith had appeared at the door with a maid and a small handbag. She'd been well aware that she hadn't been invited and had burned with shame of it.

"Algernon," Aunt Agatha said sourly. "I trust that you continue to be useless and too-often drunk."

"Hello dear Aunt," Algernon said, smiling charmingly. "The last time I saw sweet Violet, she was in her cups. As for me, I suppose I am yet the same. Father sends his regrets at missing your little party. He couldn't get away from his business."

Aunt Agatha's head cocked to the side and her gaze darted over Algernon before she humphed and took another sip of her drink. "Did he get my letter?"

"He sent me to represent, so to speak." Algernon's smarmy smile tempted the worst in Violet and she wanted more than anything to swipe it off his face.

"That wasn't the terms of my letter," Aunt Agatha replied.

Algernon paled a little and then whined, "Aunt..."

Aunt Agatha simply rose and crossed the room as the Wakefield gentlemen entered the room.

"Who is that?" Algernon hissed to Violet.

"An old friend of Aunt Agatha and his son. Their name is Wakefield."

"Do you think she'll keep her threat?"

Violet turned to him. He didn't look much like her, though they did have the same colored hair. She'd despised him since she was 11 years old and he'd cut off her braids. "What threat?"

Algernon paused and his head jerked a little bit, and then he turned to her and said, "Didn't you get a threat?"

"I have not been threatened by Agatha. What is all this about?"

"Show up or get cut out of the will? Only me? Or Meredith too?" He cast a nasty look at Violet and then his gaze considered Meredith.

Violet touched her lips and then tucked a stray hair of her bob behind her ear. Her mind was racing, jerking ahead in leaps and bounds. She and Victor hadn't been threatened. Instead, Aunt Agatha had pled with them to show up early to their regular visit. What if they weren't suspects to Aunt Agatha? What if she trusted them? A rush of hope filled Violet. She had almost been unaware of how painful it was to be suspected by her aunt

"Well?" Algernon snapped.

"Vic and I have spent every Christmas with Aunt Agatha since our mama died. She didn't need to order us here. She knew we were coming."

Algernon snarled. "Well? Do you think she'll cut us out of the will?"

"I don't understand," Violet said. "She's always maintained that none of us should expect to inherit."

"That was always bunk," Algernon snarled. "She refused to say so we wouldn't only think of her as a pile of gold."

Jack Wakefield crossed the room to them and handed Violet a fresh drink as Algernon said, "She obviously changed her mind now that she's a foot in the grave."

Violet took the drink, smiling brightly at Jack while she shot Algie a quelling look. But she couldn't hold back her feelings. She snapped, "She's only just 60. She could live for decades. Grandfather and Aunt Agatha both."

"By Jove, I hope not," Algernon said. "I'll have to get a job soon if one of them doesn't keep their promises."

Violet gasped and Algernon stepped back, stumbling a little and then said, "Only joking, of course."

He stepped away and Violet stared at Jack Wakefield with horrified eyes. "He...seems rather drunk."

"He does indeed," the younger Mr. Wakefield said almost kindly. His gaze was sharp and penetrating, however, as he followed Algernon as he crossed the room, saying something to Theodophilus and then something else to Aunt Agatha.

"He wouldn't say such things if..."

"Yes," Mr. Wakefield said. His gaze flicked over her, but when he looked at her, she didn't feel like an injured gazelle in front of a hyena like she did with that animal Theodophilus. "Would you mind introducing me around very much? I fear my father and your aunt have left me rather at loose ends."

Violet followed his gaze to the far side of the room where Aunt Agatha and the elder Mr. Wakefield were whispering together.

"Of course." Violet's mind was reeling as she started with her friends and introduced Jack to them. He asked them all to call him Jack, and she was grateful for it. Separating the Mr. Wakefields in her head was making her a little dizzy. Or perhaps that was the alcohol and the empty stomach. Or perhaps, even worse, it was the idea that someone might be trying to kill Aunt Agatha.

Violet looked over at her aunt. Her hair was white, but it was pulled back and elegant with a jeweled comb tucked into her chignon. Agatha's earrings were long and beautiful and drew attention to her still sharp jawline. She had brilliant dark eyes, very much like Violet and Victor's. Agatha's sparkled with wit, sheer cleverness, and vibrant life despite her evident exhaustion. Aunt Agatha was a powerful woman. She rode her horses daily and played tennis often. She'd purchased a car and learned to drive it early. She even owned an airplane, though after a few lessons she'd decided to have Hargreaves learn rather than fly it herself.

"Vi?" Victor said, watching her stare at their aunt. "Are you all right, love?"

"Yes, of course," Violet answered. She smiled at Jack and their friends. Only Jack seemed to realize that she was not all right. His penetrating gaze saw rather more than she was used to from a stranger.

CHAPTER SIX

*D*inner could only be described as awkward. If the vittles weren't so very good, it would have been an entire loss. Jack was seated next to Violet, and she was too well aware of him. He was a large man—not fat—not fat at all, but his shoulder still edged into her space. On her other side was Theodophilus, who seemed to be trying to mostly hide behind Violet. Usually, the swine demanded her attention whenever she was around him, but he was focused utterly on Lila.

Jack, on the other hand, had Meredith on his other side and she was nearly silent as she examined the table. Her food ended up nearly untouched as plates were placed in front of her, the food shuffled around, and then removed.

"Do you live in London?" Jack asked. "Or perhaps with your family in the country?"

"Oh," Violet smiled at him and then said, "I'm afraid my father and stepmother rather despair of my unwillingness to live with them. Victor and I share rooms in London."

Somewhere between the fish and the entrée, Meredith sighed into her wine glass and Jack turned to her, leaving Violet unattended for a moment. Her gaze darted around the room and she suddenly remembered who the man in the pinstripe suit was. John Davies—Agatha's husband's nephew. No wonder he hadn't been reintroduced. They'd shared a few holidays together when she was quite a bit younger. He'd been off to war for much of her school days and she hadn't seen him since then. If she recalled correctly, he'd been in supplies with his father helping more from behind the scenes.

It was possible full eternities had passed by the time dinner was over. The roast was moist, the wine flowed freely, and by the time little cakes were served, Violet wanted to run screaming from the dining room. The idea that someone would kill Aunt Agatha for money she'd never revealed who was receiving was shocking. Could it be true?

She'd watched her cousin, Meredith during dinner. She'd seemed the same as ever, a little too solemn, a little too sour. Surely no changes in Meredith's behavior, despite the long gap in visits meant that Meredith was unaware of the undercurrents and not plotting murder?

What about Algernon? He had always assumed he'd receive an inheritance from Aunt Agatha. An allowance too, as Violet recalled. When they were at Oxford, every time she'd come across him he'd made some comment about being poorer than expected and having thought Aunt Agatha wouldn't have been so stingy.

Was his expectation of money moving things along for him? Had he decided to escalate her death to inherit early? He *had* referred to the vibrant Aunt Agatha as having one foot in the grave. Was it her white hair and few wrinkles that prompted that or was it that he was imagining the benefits her death might bring?

Violet glanced over John Davies. He had chatted with Aunt Agatha as though they'd been in contact all of these years. Knowing Aunt Agatha, they had been. She'd probably written to him often while he served during the war and helped him get established in whatever career he was pursuing currently. Did he expect to inherit? He was the male heir of her husband and often money followed that blood line. Had John been threatened to arrive for the holidays or else? If so, was he angry about it?

Violet followed the ladies to the drawing room while her brother winked at her and lit a cigar. She shot him a quelling look and decided that a gin rickey might be what she needed to get through the evening.

By the time the cheese tray had been set to the side, the tea cart had been rolled in, and cocktails were made, the gentlemen had come in. Violet selected coffee rather than tea or a cocktail. She was seated in a corner, sipping her coffee as Victor approached.

"Victor," Violet hissed, "Distract Algernon and his hound."

Victor didn't even ask why, just made himself a drink and then offered cocktails to the others, calling Theodophilus and Algie by name. Victor started a story of a light-fingered dancing girl who'd tried to take his cigarette case and got Meredith and John Davies to join in with drinks of their own.

With their friends joining Victor, Violet was able to approach her aunt, unencumbered by listening ears.

"Aunt Agatha," Violet said, "May I get you a sherry? Or would you like to live a little and try a grasshopper? Maybe a stinger?" Violet grinned at her aunt, and tucked her arm through hers, squeezing a little. "Why not try something new?"

"Just a sherry, darling," Aunt Agatha said, squeezing Violet back.

"Mr. Wakefield?" The elder Mr. Wakefield nodded at Violet, his expression solemn. The two of them were seated side by side and seemed happy in their chatting, but Violet wouldn't be able to rest until she knew more about Aunt Agatha's worry that someone was trying to kill her. Did Mr. Wakefield know Aunt Agatha's worries? Did he believe someone was trying to kill her? *What* had happened to make Aunt Agatha scared? By Jove, Violet wanted it to all be a faradiddle.

"A sherry is fine," Mr. Wakefield said with an expressionless face. He was so impassive, Violet wasn't sure he'd react if a pig took flight right in that room.

Violet grinned, forcing a bright expression, and crossed to the drink cart while Victor led the others out the French doors to the garden. He winked as he passed her and promised the others a sight for sore eyes.

Violet noted that Algernon had managed to drink so much wine throughout the long dinner that he'd climbed to new heights of drunkenness and had been easily led, unusual for him to say the least. She checked for Theodophilus, concerned he'd stayed behind to catch her, but the room was empty except for Hargreaves silently collecting an empty port glass and putting out a still smoking cigar.

Violet wished she could shoo the elder Mr. Wakefield after the others, so she could grab a private word with Aunt Agatha, but it seemed she'd have to wait to hunt up her aunt later that evening. That might be better, as Aunt Agatha always lingered over her makeup and dressing. Many an evening had been spent with Violet brushing Agatha's hair.

"Thank you dear," Aunt Agatha said as Violet handed them both drinks. Mr. Wakefield lifted his to his mouth as Violet stepped back. He sniffed and then a shocked expression came over his face. He grabbed Agatha's drink and snarled, "Bitter almonds."

"What?" Violet gasped. "What? No!"

Terror for her aunt struck Violet speechless and frozen like a mouse before a snake. Bitter almonds? Bloody hell, it couldn't be!

Aunt Agatha took her drink back from Mr. Wakefield, lifting it to her nose, breathing deeply and then she said, "Yes. Certainly bitter almonds."

Aunt Agatha's voice was flat and her face was shocked as her gaze fell on Violet's. There was a look of reproach and, could it be, suspicion in Agatha's face.

"But...I would never." Violet's mind stumbled. Shock, more than anything else, made her utterly useless. Bitter almonds! Bitter almonds delivered by Violet's own hand. What madness was this?

"I hadn't thought you would," Aunt Agatha said, her emphasis on the past tense. "I *had* thought that you of all people could be trusted."

"I wouldn't!" Violet's hands were shaking. She wanted to sniff the drinks for herself. How had this happened? Could it be true? "Of course I wouldn't."

"There's rather a lot of money on the line," Mr. Wakefield said. "I hear that people have bets placed that you're her heir. That is rather a lot of motive isn't it? All Agatha's money is quite compelling even for the most virtuous of souls."

Violet slowly licked her lips, her brain stuttering back to life. "I may not be the most virtuous of souls nor do I claim to be a saint; however, I have no expectations that I am Aunt Agatha's heir. I have not bet on her death. Nor have I bet on her will." Each statement was said precisely. "To be perfectly clear, if I wanted money, I could get it without descending to murder."

"It's so easy, then?" Mr. Wakefield demanded, grabbing Violet's arm. "If only the rest of the world knew how easy it was to acquire money. Hargreaves, my son."

"Of course, sir, but if I may..." Hargreaves stepped forward quietly.

Violet cut in, "Aunt Agatha, you know well that I could simply accept Tomas's offer. I wouldn't have to kill my favorite aunt to be rolling in the green. Jewels, cars, money, they could all be mine by giving myself to a man I care very much for."

"That is true, James," Aunt Agatha said. She sounded as if she'd been beaten down. Violet's eyes welled in tears for her aunt. How was this happening? To her aunt of all people? She had always been generous with their family, seeing to their education, sharing her home, taking them on trips.

"If I may," Hargreaves said again, politely cutting in, this time with more insistence.

Mr. Wakefield and Aunt Agatha turned to Hargreaves who said simply, "Most everyone knows that Mrs. Davies drinks sherry after dinner. It's been her pattern for years. A glass before dinner. A second after. I believe, in fact, Violet is the only one who has persuaded you to try other drinks."

"That ghastly grasshopper the last time you were here," Aunt Agatha admitted. Her dark eyes were fixed on Violet's face and Violet was staring back, searching the face of the woman she loved so well. Was it too easy to destroy years of love?

"Indeed," Hargreaves said. "I believe you have been gifted several types of alcohol from your niece as a running joke between you."

"That is true." Aunt Agatha turned again to Violet as if searching for guilt. The sight of it was painful beyond understanding.

"It's well known, ma'am," Hargreaves inserted. "Miss Violet's teasing ways have, in fact, drawn attention to the fact that you always drink sherry. Just last month, one of the new servants was dismissed for sampling the port. He thought he could get away with it if he left your sherry alone. I believe it is presumptuous to jump to the culprit being Miss Violet. The drink cart has been unattended much of the day. Anyone could have added the cyanide to the sherry decanter."

Mr. Wakefield crossed to the decanter where the sherry was housed and breathed deeply. "Bitter almonds. Does no one else drink this?"

"Very rarely, sir," Hargreaves answered. "Mrs. Davies stocks her bar with the modern drinks and the young people almost always choose those. If someone wanted to poison just Mrs. Davies the sherry is an... excellent choice. The only thing unusual about the sherry is that Miss Violet made Mrs. Davies a different drink before dinner. If Miss Violet had not done so, perhaps we would have lost Mrs. Davies before dinner."

"The sherry is a terrible choice! Poisoning is a terrible choice!" Violet snapped. She hadn't wanted to believe that this thought of murder was real. She had wanted to believe, instead, that Aunt Agatha might have become imaginative in her advanced age. It would be far better than someone stealing Violet's aunt away. "Why would anyone poison you? It doesn't make sense."

"For the money," Aunt Agatha said simply. "Don't be simple."

"But you have never named your heir. Killing you is a gamble for money that you could have easily left to a house for wayward girls."

"The general presumption is that I have enough money to spread among all of you. Among much of the family it is well known that my husband didn't believe in leaving money outside of the family except for servants or smaller gifts."

"Is it? I didn't know that." Violet stepped back and shook her head. "You aren't going to die, Aunt Agatha. Why did you call us all here? If someone is trying to kill you, why not take a trip? Hire someone to find out who and spend some time in the sun."

"I did advise that," Mr. Wakefield said, looking no less suspicious. It was as if he wanted her to be guilty. Or perhaps he thought she was just an excellent play actress. She was, in fact, a pretty good liar, but she rarely employed the talent. "Hargreaves, get my son. Do it on the sly."

"Of course, sir."

"Please, Aunt Agatha," Violet said. "Please. Just pack your bags and go somewhere nice. You liked Greece as a girl. Go again. Rent some place by the sea and let it warm you up. What about your house on the Amalfi coast? That's a lovely place to spend the winter. Go enjoy the sun and we'll figure out who is doing this before you return."

"I'm not running," Aunt Agatha said. "I'll be damned if I flee a cowardly poisoner. I didn't make my fortune just for some scoundrel to try to steal it from me in my old age."

"No!" Violet led her aunt to a chair and seated her before dropping onto her knees in front of her. Violet took Aunt Agatha's hands and said, "You escape first and live. Then find vengeance later while you're living the high life. It is not cowardice to be smart."

"She's not wrong, Agatha," Mr. Wakefield said. "Ah...here's Jack."

Violet glanced over her shoulder and saw the massive Jack in the doorway. He took in the scene and then rather than crossing to them, he said something low to Hargreaves who nodded several times and then took the drink cart from the drawing room.

"Where are the others, my boy?" Mr. Wakefield asked.

"Victor Carlyle is telling them a ghost story."

Violet laughed a rather wet laugh and then said, "Please Agatha? Won't you please just leave? Let us figure it out for you? Victor and I will stay and help Mr. Wakefield. Whatever you need to feel like you aren't running and just taking your life back."

"I am no coward," Aunt Agatha stated. "I'll be damned if some blighter thinks he or she can come into my home like a cuckoo in the nest and eat my vittles and drink my booze and snuggle their way into my will only to stab me in the back!"

"But at least you'd be alive!" Violet shouted, losing patience.

"Alive and a coward!"

"Better than dead!"

"Is it?"

"Yes!" Violet said, "Haven't we lost enough? Mama and Peter and Lionel and baby Iris and then you? I'd rather you lived!"

"Well you're not me, girl. I don't want to just live. I want to live proud of my actions."

Violet shoved herself to her feet and said, "Isn't that clear! I would rather be smart and safe than send my loved ones through another round of loss and mourning!"

She glanced at the others and said, "I'm going to my room. If you need me, you know where I'll be. Do me a favor, Aunt. Don't die."

Violet slammed out of the room and ran up the stairs into her room. Her hands were shaking, and she wasn't sure what to do. How could someone think that killing Aunt Agatha was worth any cost? They weren't even sure who was in the will. Even if the others knew that Aunt Agatha wasn't going to leave the money to some hospital, that didn't mean that person would inherit.

Violet grabbed her pillow and beat it against the bed for several minutes, but it did no good. Oh! She needed to be able to be a man and just give something a good knuckle sandwich.

Violet locked her bedroom door and made her way to the bath. She placed the stopper in the bath and started the water. While the bath filled, Vi used her cold cream to remove her makeup. Once her face was clear, she dropped her robe, added bath salts, and slid into the water. Her mind was skittering through possibilities as she relaxed into the hot water.

Her and Victor's letter from Aunt Agatha hadn't said anything about being left out of the will. Was that because she and Victor hadn't been suspects, or because Aunt Agatha had known they'd come either way and didn't need to threaten them? Aunt Agatha certainly hadn't objected when Mr. Wakefield had assumed that Violet was trying to poison them both.

Had Agatha truly thought that Violet would try to murder her so openly? Just handing them a cup of poison and then batting her lashes to whatever detective showed up? Surely Aunt Agatha knew Violet wasn't quite so thick. Had Aunt Agatha just been startled and afraid? It felt like Violet's own mother had thought her capable of murder. She didn't want it to be true—that Agatha could think such things of her—but maybe she was wrong.

Violet finished her bath, toweling her hair dry as quickly as possible. With the short bob, it didn't take too long to dry. Rubbing cream into her body, she dressed, putting on both a nightgown and a dressing gown before she worked on her hair again. By the time she'd arranged a turban over her locks to keep them straight, there was a knock on her door. She had thought perhaps it would be Agatha or Victor, but it was Jack Wakefield.

"Oh," she said lamely, startled to see him at her bedroom door. "I..."

"I'm sorry to bother you, Lady Carlyle," he said. "Especially so late."

"Please call me Violet." She glanced down at herself and then shrugged. Her dressing gown was one of those monstrous things that was good for frigid castles and covered her from her neck to her toes. "What can I do for you?"

"I would like to talk to you about what happened with the sherry."

Violet paused, considering him, and then slowly stepped back, letting him into her room. She left the door half-open for a shade of propriety and then examined him. He'd changed since dinner. His clothes were the same, but gone was the flirtatious light in his eyes. Something cold was there instead.

"Why you?" she asked

"We weren't invited by accident, you know. I have worked for Scotland Yard as a Chief Inspector. I was also in the military police during the war. When your aunt needed help, she remembered that and asked my father and I to come visit and see if we could sort out what was happening."

"So you're here to find the would-be killer?"

He nodded and she gestured to the two chairs in front of the fire. Jack crossed and took a seat as he said, "My father and I overheard the conversation on the train regarding Mrs. Davie's will."

Violet paled at that and bit her lip. She had to admit that looked bad. Her brother keeping that book was hardly a good thing in the face of these attempted murders. She sighed and said, "Look...it isn't what it seems."

"It isn't a betting book about the death of someone?" He didn't seem to like her half-explanation, and she didn't blame him. It wasn't what he thought, but it also wasn't as bad as it seemed.

"Well. No. It is...it just...Victor started that when we were children. Perhaps fourteen?"

"But he still carries it? He's hardly fourteen anymore and far past the age when he could claim the foibles of the schoolroom."

"He dabbles in writing." They both did, but it was neither here nor there. "Victor asks questions like that all the time, keeping track of people's answers and using them to fuel his stories. He keeps those pages at the beginning of the notebook he carries along with any other notes he's taken from similar questions. Things he hasn't used in a story yet. It's habit. Not some nefarious *scheme.*"

No one knew that Victor—and Violet—were behind the stories that were published in the *The Story-Teller* magazine under the name V.V. Twinning. They published often and had quite a little following for their pseudonym.

"Are you so sure of that, Violet? I know he's your brother. Perhaps you don't see him as he is."

"He's my twin," Violet shot back. "I know him better than I know myself. I could look at him and tell you if he wanted coffee or tea. I could tell you his reaction to a picture show before he'd seen it. I could tell you if he'd like a lady before he'd met her. He would never, ever hurt Aunt Agatha. Both of us see her as our...near mother."

She rose and paced in front of the fire while Jack watched her from his place nearby. His gaze was too sharp, too likely to notice any stumble. He was too likely to pick up clues even from things that shouldn't be seen in a nefarious light.

Jack cleared his throat and then said, "His man stocked the drink cart when he arrived. Giles? He said that your brother brought rather a lot of sherry for your aunt."

"I did," Violet shot back. "Victor might have ensured it got here, but I bought it for her. I bought her a whole case when Victor and I went to Spain last summer. We..." Violet found a tear on her cheek, wiped it away with a frustrated gesture, and said, "I met this gentlemen who owned a vineyard at a party. Victor and I and our friend Tomas went and visited the vineyard and sampled his wines, and I was gifted a selection of wines from this man. I bought a case of sherry just for Agatha. Even I liked that one, and I don't care for sherry, really. But Aunt Agatha loves it. Victor and I always look for some for her if we're somewhere where it might be a little different."

"So you are responsible for the sherry served this evening?"

"I am," Violet said. "But *just* the sherry. I certainly didn't add bitter almonds to it."

"Yet you delivered it to her," he said carefully.

That sharp, penetrating gaze was on her face. She felt as if he could read her very soul. She hoped he could. Her and Victor's. As much as she wanted this to all be a mistake, she would throw Algernon and Meredith to the wolves in a shred of a moment for Victor. "I did. Anyone, however, could have."

"Do you often bring her sherry?"

"Every time we come, Victor or I will make sure Agatha has her sherry after dinner. It's him as often as I. It's been years since we've been here with the others, but I wouldn't be surprised if they did the same when they visited."

"Do the others know your habits?"

Violet paused in her pacing and said, "I don't know. Victor and I aren't close with Algie or Meredith. I didn't even recognize John at first. I haven't seen Meredith in years. I know she visits Aunt Agatha every summer. Victor and I used to as well. Lately we are only regular in our visits at Christmas. We tend to see her a couple more times every year, but the other visits aren't always at the same time and we haven't been here at the same time as Meredith since before she married. Sometimes we see her in London. Sometimes we join her when she goes to Italy. Sometimes we meet up in Bath. It's never the same outside of Christmas."

"When was the last time you saw Algernon?"

"Oh, well we see him often enough in London. We have overlapping friends. But here? I haven't seen him here since before we went away to school as children. Longer than Meredith probably."

"I understand that Theodophilus Smythe-Hill is your cousin Algernon's friend? And you and Victor brought Miss Gwyneth Walker, and Mr. and Mrs. Halicourt?"

Violet sighed and said, "When Vic and I heard that Algie was bringing Theodophilus we conscripted our friends to help provide buffer."

"Buffer?"

"Algie has a rather inflated opinion of his ability to influence who I might marry and Theo has an eye on what I can offer him."

"What can you offer him?"

"Connections and money. Of late, he's been more and more overt in his pursuit. Somehow even finding whichever parties or restaurants that Victor and I might patronize. It feels very...deliberate."

Jack stood, towering over Violet and she shivered. She'd liked the way he made her feel delicate before, but now that she was a suspect and he was the investigator, she felt rather like a mouse before the lion.

"It was my understanding that those of you here are all rather in need of money. The heirs with needs and hopes."

Violet adjusted her robe and looked up at Jack. "When your father is an earl and you aren't the heir, you're poor. It is an accepted, if inaccurate fact. To be honest, in comparison to our brother, Gerald—Victor and I are paupers. The truth of the matter is that we have enough to live on without working, that we have the expectations of more, *through our father,* and that neither of us are spendthrifts. I hardly think we're all that hard up."

"Hmmm." Jack nodded to Violet, excused himself, and left her feeling as though she'd been turned inside out even though he hadn't been all that intimidating. Her soul was quaking from someone trying to kill her beloved aunt and having almost delivered the murderous blow herself. Violet took in a deep breath. She and her brother were too embroiled in the suspicion for her to be happy. The fact that a need for suspicion existed at all was her worst nightmare. Jack seemed to know what he was doing, but she didn't consider her freedom, her brother's freedom, or her aunt's life something that you left to others to protect. She'd be seeing to it herself instead.

CHAPTER SEVEN

*V*iolet left her room as soon as Jack Wakefield was gone and crossed to her brother's room. She knocked on his door and he called, "Vi?"

"How did you know it was me?"

"It's not like one of the others will come knocking at my door at night, luv." He swung the door wide and gestured to one of the two chairs in front of the fire. "Giles has arrived like a savior in the nighttime and has brought all the best things. But he did hand me this for you."

Violet took the box from Victor and found simply loads of chocolates.

"Apparently, Harold Lannister enjoyed dinner, the play, and your pretty face."

Violet had enjoyed the play but suddenly Harold was far less intriguing than he'd been before. Somehow, despite investigating her, Jack Wakefield had become the example of manhood and Harold had become a weak worm of a man. To be fair, Harold was quite slender and barely taller than Violet. She hadn't minded when they'd been at dinner and his stories had been amusing, the food had been delicious, and he'd known all the best dance steps. Now, however, he was overshadowed by the massive and too-insightful Jack Wakefield.

"It was a good play," Violet said smoothly popping a chocolate into her mouth and handing the rest to Victor. "Brother, Aunt Agatha thinks someone is trying to kill her."

Victor's gaze widened and he ran his hand through his hair. "Well... is....is that why she wanted us here? Why she demanded we rally round? Say it isn't so."

"Apparently all of her potential heirs received letters demanding their presence or they'd be cut out of the will. It's far worse than that though."

Victor choked and then cleared his throat. He stood and crossed to a table in the corner and poured himself and Violet a glass of port before he turned to the chair beside the fire.

"Why didn't she say that to us? Why threaten them and not us?"

Violet shook her head, adjusting her turban before she said, "I don't think we were real suspects until this evening."

"What happened this evening?" Victor demanded. He took a fortifying gulp of his port and leaned forward.

Violet took a sip of the port, echoing her brother's movement, but she swallowed slowly, letting it burn its way down her throat while she gathered her emotions. She didn't want to blubber on her brother's shoulder about everything. She wanted to set aside her emotions and engage her brain unencumbered by feeling. She wasn't capable of that, however. Not with Aunt Agatha at risk.

Violet took a deep breath and said, "I poured Aunt Agatha and Mr. Wakefield a glass of sherry."

Victor shrugged and raised his brows. It was so very typical of either of them to do that. He didn't need her to tell him there was more to the story.

"It was poisoned."

"By Jove! That cannot be true!"

Violet took another fortifying drink of the port and then said, "But it is. Both of them assumed I had murderous intentions until Hargreaves pointed out that everyone knew Aunt Agatha enjoyed sherry in the evening and that the decanter could be poisoned. Once they determined it was, the suspicion faded. It's not gone, however. Not at all."

Victor took her hand, setting aside his port and squeezing tightly. "Aunt Agatha was just startled. She knows you better than that, my girl."

Violet let a tear fall—with Victor she didn't have to hide herself—though Jack had too much of a glance at her soul. The problem was he thought she could be acting while Victor knew she wasn't. Victor, in fact, knew what she was feeling before she even let her feelings show. She took the handkerchief Victor offered her and curled into her seat by his fire.

"That's why the Wakefield gentlemen are here, Vic. Jack Wakefield was one of those military coves who investigate crimes in the troops. He worked for Scotland Yard too. Or does now? I don't know. I got the impression that he still may. Regardless, Aunt Agatha was afraid enough to call on them. Something else must have happened to scare her."

"Aunt Agatha afraid..." Victor mused. "It doesn't seem possible." Victor's mouth snapped shut for a moment and then he demanded, "What are they thinking? That you were going to kill her for the money?"

"I believe so. Everyone talks about us like we're paupers, you know that. Get a job, Victor. Get married, Violet. That man has a fortune. This one is the younger son of a duke. That one owns half that shipping company. Etcetera, etcetera."

"They're so worried about someone supporting you and me marrying some nice young girl and supporting her that they don't realize we're not ready for such things."

"Or that everyone we know is unhappily married. Papa and Eleanor. Gerald and Amelia. The only married couple I know that is happy is Denny and Lila."

"I know, luv. I know. I agree."

Violet rose and picked up Victor's slacks from the end of his bed, hanging them up for him. He had changed into his silk striped pajamas with a loose robe.

"Giles will do that, luv," Victor said, as if he'd said it a thousand times before. To be fair, he had. Violet had a hard time leaving things lying about she could so easily put away.

"I know," Violet said. She wasn't picking up after him out of some need to be domesticated. She was doing it to keep busy. She felt as though eyes were on her that moment. How could they be in this childhood refuge with someone who wanted to kill their aunt? It wasn't possible, was it?

Yet, she knew it was. She'd smelled those bitter almonds when given the chance. She'd seen the fear in Aunt Agatha's gaze. She'd seen the suspicion in Jack and Mr. Wakefield's. Only Hargreaves had looked beyond her after that had happened.

This need to keep moving when things were bad was probably why grandmothers were so good at embroidery. They were stifled into doing nothing and had to at least use their hands, if not their minds. So, their homes were filled with endless embroidered doo-dads.

"Victor, I want to go to America. And Greece. Or perhaps we can spend the rest of the winter on the Amalfi Coast? Please say yes."

"Yes, of course," Victor replied without hesitation. "We'll sort out Aunt Agatha, find out who is trying to kill her, murder them, maim them, and set them on fire, and then borrow her villa there. Maybe we can get her to come with us and tinker with buying some new wines. We'll write some stories about rich coves lazing about in the sun."

Violet grinned at him. They would be those rich coves. Half their stories were exaggerated accounts of their own exploits.

"You are going to need a bigger house, darling, if you keep buying so much wine."

"Dear Aunt Agatha has been letting me use her cellar. I have it all in hand, of course."

"Of course," Violet said, softly.

She arranged her brother's bottle of Brilliantine and combs. She tucked a few stray cigarettes back into their case, and then straightened the items on his table before she turned back to him and said, "What do we do, Vic? We can't let someone hurt Agatha."

He searched her face. It was quite rare for the lion inside of Victor to come out. Most of the time he was a charming spaniel, but she could see the fierceness in his matching eyes at the moment. Could she read him so well because they'd shared a womb, or was it just that they had the same eyes? Did she see the lion in him because she felt the lioness in herself?

"Agatha is brilliant. If she thinks this has to do with her will, it does. Let's just convince her to leave it all to charity and announce it. Perhaps then, whoever is trying to kill her will stop."

Violet considered. Who were the real suspects if she ruled out herself and Victor? Algernon. Meredith. John Davies. Those were the only relatives who'd arrived. Had everyone else not believed Agatha's threat, or had they already accepted they wouldn't be in the will?

"Oh, this worm!" she snarled. "We shall find him and stomp him."

"Do you not think it's a her?"

Violet considered and then shrugged. "Meredith? Maybe. Darling, we hardly know her. She's an....archetype. The poor widow. Do you know what she likes? Who her friends are? If she even has some old gals she bounces around with? To be honest, I'm not even sure where she lives."

"I have no idea," Victor admitted. "I hadn't even realized I knew nothing about the gel until you pointed it out. She's just always...Merry."

"That mean name we gave her. Do you think she realized?"

Victor winced and then asked, "That we called her Merry because she was always so dour? I have no idea. We were terrible children."

Violet sat back down across from Victor, snatching another chocolate, and then she asked, "Maybe we should just go? Just leave it to the professional Mr. Wakefield and remove ourselves from suspicion."

Victor considered along with Violet and then both shook their heads in near unison.

"We can't, luv."

"We'll never forgive ourselves if something happens to her," Violet added for them both. "We have to at least try."

Victor nodded and said, "I'll try to talk to her tomorrow and see what I can get out of Algernon. If it *is* one of us, surely something has changed? There's some spurring moment that made this happen now instead of before?"

Violet didn't know. She preferred to avoid Algie whenever possible, hadn't remembered John Davies, and felt sorry for Meredith. "I need to talk to Aunt Agatha again. I won't be able to sleep until I do."

"Be careful, darling," Victor said. "Whoever is trying to hurt Aunt Agatha has gone mad. None of us are truly safe. Stop by my room on the way back and I'll walk you to yours and wait until you're locked in."

Violet hesitated, hating the rush of fear that struck her before she nodded once and then said, "You be safe too, brother mine."

Aunt Agatha's rooms were on the other side of the house in the east wing. Violet headed through the halls alone and jumped at nearly every sound, feeling a lot like a gothic heroine who was about to be strangled in the shadows by some specter. Perhaps she and Victor should consider adventure tales instead of ghost stories.

Violet knocked lightly on Aunt Agatha's bedroom door and it opened along with the one across the hall. Inside the second room was both James and Jack Wakefield with loosened ties and pipes in their hands. Violet shot them a tight smile and stepped into Aunt Agatha's room.

She was sitting at her dressing table, slowly taking off her jewelry. She still wore a little rouge on her cheeks, but the flush from her own heightened fear or worry made her far more red than any cream makeup product.

Violet crossed to her and said, "Perhaps I won't offer to get you a drink, but may I put your jewelry up for you?"

"Martha will do it," Aunt Agatha said, voice tight. Her lips were pressed together as soon as she finished speaking.

"You know I rather like putting things away," Violet said softly and waited for her aunt's nod before she took the jewelry, opening the locked jewelry box. It was a carved, silver box with scrolled detailing. Inside, Martha had allowed it to become a jumble of bracelets, rings, and earrings. The mess made Violet's fingers itch. "Did Martha allow this to become so very unorganized just for me?"

"I doubt it," Aunt Agatha snapped. She was furious. It was evident in the tense line of her shoulders, the way her neck seemed almost brittle in its movement, the way her lips pressed together and her eyes were narrowed on Violet's face in the mirror.

"I'm not trying to kill you," Violet said, pulling out a tray of rings and taking up a cotton cloth to wipe them down and put them away properly.

Aunt Agatha said nothing as Violet carefully pulled out the jewelry, organized it by sets, and returned it to the drawers and boxes inside of the jewelry box. These were just Aunt Agatha's favorite pieces. The riches just in the box were the very reason that someone was trying to kill Aunt Agatha. Suddenly, Violet hated the sight of the shining diamonds and rubies.

"This brooch has a loose stone," Violet said, hoping that with patience and stubbornness Aunt Agatha would explain.

"I'll have to send it with Hargreaves to be fixed," Aunt Agatha said.

Violet nodded and put the piece into a velvet bag and into a compartment at the top of the jewelry box.

"This earring set is missing one," Violet said a moment later.

"Yes, I know. I lost it when I was in the garden. I had hoped it would turn up."

Violet put the pearls that Aunt Agatha had worn that evening away, carefully arranging them in their case and then said, "Won't you tell me what has been happening?"

Aunt Agatha placed her brush on her vanity table and met Violet's gaze through the mirror.

"I know you're upset and have to consider everyone who might want you dead," Violet said carefully. "Victor and I consider you a mother. I know I can only protest our innocence, but *it isn't us.*"

Violet's lips trembled and she noted that Aunt Agatha's fingers were shaking on top of her brush. She slowly curled them into a fist and placed it in her lap. This distance between them was the fault of the would-be killer, and Violet just might commit murder after all. She'd hunt up who was doing this to them and finish things.

CHAPTER EIGHT

"About two months ago, I went for my daily ride," Aunt Agatha said finally, the tension between them fading. "Someone had cut the girth and I fell. I was lucky that it gave when it did and that I wasn't jumping that day. It was pure luck, Violet. Normally my ride is through the woods as fast as Hercules can go. You know how I ride. I strained my wrist instead of breaking my neck."

"I do," Violet agreed. "You were very lucky to have not hurt yourself in the woods. If that fall hadn't killed you, the elements might have before you were found."

"I had decided to visit Hargreaves's mother that day," Aunt Agatha said, "She's been doing quite poorly and I was bringing her a basket. It was entirely out of my pattern."

Violet settled down on the cushioned stool near Aunt Agatha, feeling the rising tension. She tightened her jaw to keep a slew of curses from escaping. "Was that it, or was there more?"

"That would have been enough. It was clear that the girth had been cut, not that it was an accident."

"But," Violet prompted. She closed the newly organized jewelry box and took up Aunt Agatha's brush, working through her long hair.

"A few weeks later, I had gone for a walk. It had been storming for days beforehand, and it was the first clear day in ages. I felt as though I'd been locked inside. You know how I am after that type of weather."

"I do," Violet said. Was she the only one? Or did some of the others know how Aunt Agatha would have certainly gone for a walk after such weather?

"As usual, I went down by the stream. I love to hear the water."

"I know you do," Violet murmured, carefully smoothing her aunt's hair. "You went down to the bridge? Where we used to throw rocks in with Algie and Merry?"

Violet hated that she felt the need to point out that she was not the only one who knew about Aunt Agatha's propensity for walking there.

"Yes, there," Agatha agreed. If she noticed Violet's assertion, she didn't say anything. "The bridge has needed to be replaced for some time, but I crossed it like I always do. It was Tuesday afternoon and my book club gathers at Mrs. Lavender's home. I was walking that way for tea, gossip, and possibly talking about the book."

Violet nodded. She'd accompanied her aunt a few times on her visits.

"Someone came up behind me and shoved me into the railing. It broke, as it's been rotten for ages. Since it had been raining for days, the stream was flooded and busting with rage. I barely got out. Thankfully John Lockwood had been playing in the woods. He saw me struggle to the bank and pulled me out. He helped me home. Vi," Aunt Agatha trailed off. She shivered in her remembrance and Violet put down the brush to wrap her arms around her aunt.

"I was in bed for days. That's when I decided it was time to confront whomever was doing this to me. To find them and make them pay. That's when I came up with the plan for the holidays and James Wakefield. I left until just yesterday to protect myself. Went to Bath and didn't tell anyone except James."

Violet couldn't speak. She got up and paced around Aunt Agatha's massive rooms. There was a stack of books on Agatha's bedside table. She had a journal on her desk and there were letters stacked nearby. Violet passed by the table and caught sight of her own writing.

Violet muttered under her breath as she paced, feeling her aunt's gaze on her. Aunt Agatha slowly turned around until she faced the raging Violet, who came to stop and turned. "I didn't even know about your husband's want to leave money in the family. I thought you'd leave everything to a school or something."

Agatha sighed and then admitted, "Without Henry's wishes, I might have left everything just as you say."

"You still can," Violet told her. "Why don't you? He wouldn't want to see you murdered for that money. He loved you."

"But I can't," Agatha whispered. "You don't know what it was like in my day. In my day, a man such as Henry who saw my mind and admired it instead of feeling emasculated. We used to talk at night about how we'd create this gift for our family. It was supposed to be our children."

Aunt Agatha's face crumpled for a moment, but it smoothed out soon after. Violet dropped to her knees in front of her aunt again, taking her hands. "Henry and I worked together at making money. It was this game for us. We'd read about companies and types of investments. He always talked about building an empire for our children. A gift for them, he said. Keeping that up is what got me through the early years after his death. Since we weren't blessed with children, I just shifted our dream of the empire to you children. In many ways, you all *were* my children."

Violet felt as though that specter from the hall were chasing her through Agatha's rooms. She could almost feel the ghost of her uncle Henry, the feel of death himself, haunting the halls, the threat that someone she loved would be taken. All for what? What was supposed to have been a gift!

"Whatever money you have is not worth the risk of life in jail or being hanged!" Violet declared. "Who could be so...evil?"

"Does Tomas's marriage proposal still stand, Violet?" Aunt Agatha asked, changing the subject.

But not really changing it at all. The question stabbed Violet right through the center. She had to take a breath before she could even answer. "Yes, Aunt. Tomas hasn't withdrawn his offer. I don't imagine that he will anytime soon. He has pinned his hopes on me and probably will until I marry or he meets the right woman for him."

"I'm sorry I have to ask it," Aunt Agatha said.

"As am I."

"You are rather poor compared to many of your friends, Violet. One misstep for you or Victor and you two will have to get work. Gone will be the days of private rooms, eating at restaurants, jazz clubs, dancing, and drinking."

"We do work," Violet said, telling their secret for the first time. "We've been writing a series of stories for one of those pulp magazines. Combined with the money from Mama and the allowance from Papa, we're doing quite well."

"I wasn't aware of the writing." Agatha seemed to doubt it.

"Of course you weren't. It isn't like we've told anyone. Can you imagine my stepmother's reaction? But Victor and I have fun writing them. They're all in good fun. You know how he scribbled stories when we were younger? Somewhere along the way, I started helping."

Aunt Agatha's gaze searched Violet's and Violet said, "We both have degrees from Oxford. We could both get work. I could find work as a secretary. One of father's many chums could set Victor up. If we really wanted something different, we don't need to kill you to make it happen."

"You were never my main suspect," Aunt Agatha said. "You and Victor are the only ones who have never alluded to an inheritance or told me your story of how you need help. You've never tried to beg or borrow money. In fact, you're the only ones who show up with gifts like the sherry."

"The unpoisoned sherry," Violet added, knowing that Aunt Agatha had every reason to feel as she did. She knew that Aunt Agatha had to be careful. She'd already survived three attempts to take her life. When would her luck run out? "Must you face off with this person? Surely, with Mr. Wakefield working the case and three instances to track down, we can figure out who is doing this?"

"Like you said, Violet. None of you are *really* poor. What does it cost to pay someone to cut Hercules's girth? Or to push an old lady off a bridge?"

Violet's jaw snapped shut. She hadn't thought of that, and she ought to have. It was time to set aside the booze and the fun and focus on this dilemma.

"To be honest with you, Aunt Agatha, if someone murders you while you are determined to track them down instead of being safe, I will hold a grudge into the afterlife."

On another night, Violet would have offered to get her aunt some warm milk to help her sleep or suggest she take a little something. That wasn't something Vi could do at the moment. Not with suspicions running high. Instead, she kissed her aunt's cheek and left the bedroom.

CHAPTER NINE

*J*ack Wakefield stepped out his bedroom as Violet stepped out of Agatha's. It seemed he had been waiting for her.

"Did you want to ensure she yet lives?"

His jaw tightened and Violet, in a spur of anger, threw open her aunt's door and called, "Have you been stabbed, aunt?"

"No, you indomitable brat."

"Have I given you anything to drink? Or slipped a snake into your bedsheets?"

"We chatted and she left, Jack. Thank you for checking on me."

"Lock your door," Jack said, reaching in with one hand and an averted gaze to close Aunt Agatha's door. He waited until he heard the lock click and tested it before he turned to Violet. "She asked me to rule out you and Victor first. She told me she doesn't really believe it is you, but feels she has to be sure."

"Wonderful. Fabulous. We're suspected, but less so. I wish I could say that made me feel better."

"It should. Your aunt didn't want to suspect you at all, but felt like you needed to be ruled out."

"I feel like you just reworded what I just said." Violet fisted her hands and wished she could pound on something with them, but she was too well schooled in manners to hit him or the wall.

Instead she gritted her teeth and sped up her walk. Jack followed without a problem. If anything, he was just walking normally now with his giant legs while she was skipping along like a tiny dog next to a horse.

"Perhaps," he said calmly.

Oh! She wanted to just turn and give him a good shove. It would probably be like shoving against a mountain. Useless and foolish.

"Why are you following me?"

"I am ensuring you arrive at your room safely."

She shot him an infuriated glance, darted down the stairs of the east wing and up the stairs of the west wing. She stopped at her brother's door, pounding her fist against it.

The clicking of his typewriter cut off and he opened the door.

"Hullo, darling," he said, and then scowled at Jack.

"I'm fine. Mr. Wakefield has determined to ensure that I neither murder anyone on the way to my rooms or am murdered by Aunt Agatha's tormentor."

Jack growled at the back of his throat and Victor's gaze widened, darting between the massive Jack and the much smaller form of his twin.

"Well...I....do you really think it's quite the thing to antagonize the sleuth, luv?"

Violet's answer was to leave her brother and Jack standing in the hall and cross to her own room, slamming the door in their faces.

"Lock the door," Jack called.

She stomped her foot since no one could witness it and then turned the lock. A moment later he tested her door handle and then all was silent. If her brother made a comment, she didn't hear it. Violet crossed to the bathroom door and locked it as well. Gwennie had the room on the other side of the bath, but Violet wasn't going to be taking chances with her life.

Before she went to bed, Violet listed out all of the family members both present and those who were not, and who might feel like they had a claim on Aunt Agatha's wealth. Given that she and Victor were related to Agatha through their dead mother, at least none of their siblings were on the list.

It read:

JOHN DAVIES — Henry Davies's only nephew. If Henry had survived, would John be the heir? Does he believe he is the heir? If so, has he run out of money or been disinherited? Why would he suddenly decide to kill his aunt? Have there been any material changes in his life?

ALGERNON ALLYN — Agatha's great nephew. Child of Kingsley Allyn. The only one of Kingsley's children to arrive, though the rest are still in the schoolroom. Always been too focused on Agatha's money. He seemed to know about Uncle Henry's desire to leave the money in the family. When had he learned what she and Victor hadn't known?

CECIL — next child of Kingsley Allyn. Only 15 years old. Unlikely killer.

AGATHA — only daughter of Kingsley Allyn. Only 11 years old. Named after Aunt Agatha deliberately. Unlikely killer.

MEREDITH ALLYN —Agatha's great niece. Cecil Allyn's child. Seems pretty hard up. Spends time with Agatha every year and knows her well. Her material status doesn't seem to have changed much. Could she really have decided after all this time to kill?

CHRISTINE ALLYN-JENNINGS — Agatha's great niece. Cecil Allyn's child. She is the favored child of Cecil. Never been one of the cousins who spent so much time with Agatha. Of the sisters, surely she doesn't expect much, if anything, from Aunt Agatha?

CECIL ALLYN.—Agatha's brother. They haven't spoken in years. Surely, he doesn't expect to inherit. Unlikely killer.

KINGSLEY ALLYN— Agatha's brother. No love lost here either. But they aren't estranged. He received the threatening letter about the inheritance and didn't show. Does he already not expect to inherit? Did he think sending Algernon was enough? Doesn't he have his own fortune?

To be fair, Violet made entries for herself and her brother. It made her angry to do it, but she decided to humor Aunt Agatha's own fears.

VIOLET CARLYLE —Agatha's great niece. Partially raised by

Aunt Agatha. An heir? Maybe. Has money from her own mother and father and doesn't need to murder for money. Let alone has an offer of marriage from Tomas St. Marks who is simply floating in money. She'd sooner cut off her own hands than murder her aunt. Never expected to inherit over John Davies or her male cousins.

VICTOR CARLYLE — Agatha's great nephew. Partially raised by Aunt Agatha. An heir? Over John Davies? Surely that's unlikely. Victor has money from both parents and doesn't need to murder. Couldn't get away with eating breakfast without Violet knowing, let alone plotting murder. Him a murderer? Never.

Violet didn't sleep so much as explore the far corners of her bed as she tossed and turned. When the servants started moving around, she was already sitting on the window seat with her list of suspects in her lap. She rose and made her way down the stairs. She was a little surprised to find Algernon already in the breakfast room. When Hargreaves entered, Algernon handed him a sheet of paper and said, "Send someone with it right away."

"Of course, sir," Hargreaves said.

Violet followed him out the door and into the hall where they were alone. "Hargreaves," she said quietly.

He turned. "Miss?"

"Do you know if any of my cousins knows the details of Aunt Agatha's will?"

His jaw tightened and his gaze flitted over her face. "I have never suspected you, miss. I encouraged Mrs. Davies to call on you and Victor for help."

"Thank you, Hargreaves. That means more than you know."

He nodded and said, "I was there when the will was made. I was, in fact, one of the witnesses when your aunt signed it. No one from the family was present. A clerk from the law office provided the second necessary witnessing signature."

Violet pressed her lips together and thought for a moment. "Do you know where it is kept?"

He nodded.

"Do you know if anyone else knows where it is kept?"

Hargreaves paused, considering for a moment and then said, "That I cannot say, miss."

"Think on it, will you? I don't expect you to tell me where it is. But see if you can remember anyone being found near it. I assume it's been safely put away."

Hargreaves nodded and then said, "I will think on it and ask the others. Mrs. Davies changed it within the year, so...perhaps we can narrow this down."

"Thank you, Hargreaves."

Violet retuned to the breakfast room. "Good morning," she said to Algernon.

Then she made her way to the loaded side table overflowing with breakfast for the early risers. Violet poured herself a cup of strong black tea and took a few slices of toast before she sat down across from her cousin. "Algie."

"Vi," he replied with a sharp nod. He had a newspaper at his side, but hadn't opened it yet. "Sleep well?"

"No, indeed not. You?"

He shot her a rather unreadable look and took a drink of his tea. "Odd to be here again like this ,isn't it? Rather like the old days when we played in the stream and rode Aunt Agatha's horses."

"I suppose so," she said, wondering if he'd heard rumors about someone trying to kill Aunt Agatha. Surely the servants had figured it out. If they had, then it would reach the others soon enough. That was the way things worked with servants. There were no secrets. "It's rather odd to be around Meredith again. It's been far longer than I'd realized."

"She's still a dour thing, isn't she?" Algie laughed. "Always had a touch of the blue to her. Had to be awkward having her father shove her off on Agatha like he did."

"She is a widow, Algie," Violet reminded him. "Meredith rather has a reason to be a bit blue, doesn't she?"

"Come now. It's been years since her husband died. Heard it was something of a whirlwind romance. He lived just long enough to spend the money grandfather left her. What about you? Do you still have the money grandfather left you or did you and Victor fritter it away?"

Violet paused to take a long sip of her tea and examine her cousin. He was asking with a purpose, wasn't he? "Why ever do you care, cuz?"

Algernon flushed a bit and then said, "I suppose it was a bit out of the way to ask you that, wasn't it?"

"A bit," she said. She would have to set Victor on the hunt about why Algie was inquiring into her finances.

"You think you're Aunt Agatha's heir?" he asked as Jack Wakefield entered the breakfast room. Suddenly those sharp eyes were fixed on her while Algie hadn't even realized that they had company beyond the footman standing near the sideboard.

"I have no reason to presume I am. I suppose any of us could be. My bet, if I were callous enough to make one, would be on John Davies."

"Why?" Algie demanded. "Didn't you know that the investment money Aunt Agatha and Henry used to build their fortune was from grandfather? Surely one of Aunt Agatha's blood will inherit?"

"I have no idea who her heir is," Violet admitted to Algie. "I never thought too much about it, to be honest."

"Come now," Algie scoffed, "Why do you spend so much time with her then?"

"I love her, you twit! My mama asked Agatha to look after Victor and me. She cared for us through our childhoods for Mama."

"Oh yes," Algie said as Jack took the seat next to Violet. "I forgot your mama foisted you two off on Agatha. Rather clever of your mum to put you in the way of Agatha like that."

Violet dropped her toast and pushed her plate away. She leaned forward, ignoring Jack Wakefield to hiss, "My mother knew she was dying and wanted someone to love us and look out for us. It wasn't about Agatha's money. It was about her heart. You are a worm, Algernon Allyn, and you always have been."

She stood and strode to the door, chased out by Algie's aside to Jack: "Women! They never are rational, are they? Not sure giving them the vote was quite the thing. Even if she can't vote for a while yet."

Violet slammed the door to the breakfast room in answer to that nonsense.

CHAPTER TEN

*V*iolet rushed from the breakfast room and flew through the halls, moving for the sake of moving rather than with any particular destination in mind. When Theodophilus stepped from the shadows near the billiards room, Violet shrieked a little.

"Didn't mean to scare you, sweet one," he said.

"Do not refer to me by endearments," she told him, taking a step back as he took a step forward.

"But I feel endearing towards you, *my* sweet." An oily smile spread over his face with too much snake in it for Violet's taste.

She stopped backing up, because she refused to be cornered. "Be that as it may, you may call me Miss Carlyle or Lady Violet if you prefer." The reference to her title was intentional. She wasn't a snob but if the recollection of her father, the earl, got Theodophilus to back up, she'd allow class snobbery to interfere.

"Violet, sweet," he said. "I think we're rather past that. You're getting a bit long in the tooth, aren't you? Won't be long before you have to take down your airs and realize that the men have moved on to younger prey than you. Your options are waning."

"Wonderful," Violet snapped. "The men will have moved on, and we'll all get what we want."

"But I won't, sweet," he said, taking a strand of her hair and tugging it too hard. It was as if he were trying to pretend to romance but the monster inside didn't allow the lie. "I want you."

"No," she said flatly.

"I'd heard all the stories about when women say no," Theodophilus said. "Your cousin said you'd be willing. Said you were getting desperate. Women say no to engender further asking, further chasing. It is a game you play, is it not?"

Violet laughed into his face and he took her by the shoulders, shoving her against the wall. "Are you laughing at me, sweet?" The word sweet was suddenly a threat instead of a pet name, and she had to fight a shiver.

"Women sometimes say no because they mean it, Mr. Smythe-Hill. You've been misled. Algie has very little idea of what I want."

"Algie has very little idea about many things. How much do you care for your cousin?"

"Why?" she asked, trying to twist out of his grasp. He was squeezing her shoulders so tightly she would be bruised, but she would be damned if she'd cry out for the bloody fiend. "Let me go."

"You need to think about how much you love your cousin. And how much trouble you want to see him in."

"Let me go," she demanded, refusing to listen to his threats.

"He's in rather a lot of trouble."

"So will you be. Let me go at once!"

He shook her and someone cleared a throat behind them.

Violet turned and saw Hargreaves's niece, Beatrice. The fear Violet had been trying to hide came flooding forward. Her gaze was pleading with the girl, hopefully she was bright enough to stay.

"Later, girl," Theodophilus snapped. "We are having a private conversation."

"Let me go," Violet said, distinctly, hoping—once again—that Beatrice was made of stern enough stuff to stick with Violet.

"I said later, girl," Theodophilus snapped again, squeezing Violet even harder.

"I'm afraid not, sir," Beatrice said consolingly. "Miss, Mrs. Davies has asked for you."

Theodophilus let Violet go, hissing into her ear as he did, "We'll speak of this again."

"Stay away from me," she said clearly.

"We're not finished," he replied, grabbing her harder before letting her go and almost floating down the hallway.

"Do you believe that? Assaulting me in my aunt's house and then just gliding away as if he weren't a snake with slicked back hair and new money."

Typically speaking, Violet wasn't one to turn up her nose at anyone, let alone a family who'd pulled themselves out of the middle class to the wealthy, but she was willing to make an exception for that animal.

"Are you all right, miss?" Beatrice's eyes flooded with tears for Violet who had to look away or cry as well.

"I'm fine," she lied. Just yesterday she'd been admiring how it felt somehow good to be small next to Jack Wakefield. Yet, Theodophilus had just made her feel helpless and he was a Lilliputian compared to Jack. She took in a fortifying breath and pasted a calm expression on her face.

"Did you need me to send for your brother?" Beatrice asked carefully. She was clearly too sharp to pull the wool over her eyes. It wasn't surprising given Hargreaves's superior brainwork. It must run in the family.

"Indeed not." Violet crossed her arms over her chest. "Did my aunt really need me?"

"I am afraid that was a little fabrication," Beatrice replied. "I hope that I did the right thing."

"You did, indeed," Violet said. "Thank you."

The gratitude was both for the lie and for the care in her voice. Violet ran up the stairs at the back of the house, not caring that she was on the servant's case. She went directly to her brother's room. Slamming open the door, she called his name, entirely uncaring of the unmoving heap of him on the bed. She called him again and poured herself a generous glass of port.

"Go away, Giles. We're on holiday."

"Wake up, you lazy lout," Violet snapped, throwing a brush her brother's way and taking a seat by the fire.

"It's not the thing to just burst into my room, Vi. You're the devil."

"Algernon asked me if I'd frittered away my inheritance from Grandfather at breakfast," Violet said, rising to yank her brother's covers off. She averted her eyes and swallowed a massive gulp of the port and then choked on it.

"So?" Victor asked, slowly pushing up. "I'm tired, sister. I wrote for hours last night."

"And then that snake, Theodophilus, manhandled me in the hallway and insinuated that I was his for the taking as some sort of recompense for something between himself and Algie."

Victor was silent, but he sat up slowly, then swung his legs over the side of his bed. His gaze had sharpened as he took in her disheveled hair, her too-bright eyes, her shaking hands, and the alcohol.

He cleared his throat and asked, "What now?"

Violet saluted him with her port and answered, "You heard me, brother."

"Assaulted you?"

"I'll be wearing gowns with sleeves for a week or two." Violet rubbed her shoulder, still feeling the press of Theodophilus's fingers into her skin, the way she'd been unable to get away. "Hargreaves's niece rescued me. Found us and made up a story about Aunt needing me. The girl refused to leave until he let me go."

"What now?" Victor demanded again, making Violet repeat it all. He cross-examined her for details and exact language. She repeated her story, including what she'd learned of Aunt Agatha's near misses the previous evening.

When he stood, he was no longer her lazy spaniel brother. Victor refilled her glass and drank most of it himself. "Go to your room. I'll send Lila or Gwennie your way. Stay with them, Violet. I mean it."

She didn't argue, though she'd be damned if she'd let him tell her what to do. She was the older twin and she didn't see how his being a male somehow made him more capable. On the average day, her brother would tell anyone that she was the useful twin, and he was lucky she'd been around to keep him out of trouble. Today wasn't going to change that.

She did remember, however, that flash of vulnerability. The way she'd been unable to get away from Theodophilus. The way he'd deliberately dug his fingers into her shoulders, knowing he was stronger than her and that there was nothing she could do. And then she nodded. She'd go to her room and let Victor handle this. A wise retreat to leave Victor to the manhandling while she plotted for them both.

CHAPTER ELEVEN

*G*wennie and Lila knocked on Violet's door by the time she'd rung the bell, requested two hot compresses, and laid herself on the bed with a warm cloth over her eyes. She'd stripped herself down to her slip, put on her silk kimono, and curled onto her bed.

Beatrice had brought the compresses along with tea, fussing over Violet until she had her feet up. The maid stayed behind and when the knock came, she answered the door.

Despite the fussing, spiders had taken roost in Violet's stomach and they didn't fade with the tea, the compresses, or the company. She'd even tried mentally conjugating Latin verbs to no avail.

"Is it true, darling? Did that beast hurt you?" Gwennie asked. She crossed to Violet, examined her setup and then sat on the end of the bed without adjusting any of Beatrice's good work.

Lila simply bypassed asking questions and crossed to where Violet had the hot compresses on her shoulders and pulled them away.

"That's going to bruise." Lila frowned as she said, "Denny and Victor are taking care of it. Even jolly Denny was enraged. He had rather a lot of things to say and none of them are repeatable."

Beatrice silently poured tea, not saying a word as Gwennie moaned for Violet and Lila raged against Theodophilus, his ancestry, and the stupidity of Algernon in getting mixed up with *that type*.

Violet was started to move past that and onto something else. She wanted to know *why* Theodophilus thought he could just force her into something and vaguely threaten Algernon at the same time. Weren't they chums? Didn't they go out and about the town together? Didn't they almost live in each other's pockets?

"What is this?" Lila demanded. She picked up Violet's list of suspects for Aunt Agatha and read it aloud.

"Attempted murderer suspects? Unlikely? Violet, is this one of your and Victor's games?"

Violet sat slowly up. She hadn't intended to tell Gwennie and Lila about that.

"But...it has you and Victor on it. Is this real? Violet, *what* is going on?"

Violet took a slow sip of her tea, eyed Beatrice and decided against telling the girl to leave. Instead Violet said, "It's why we were called here. Girls...someone is trying to kill Aunt Agatha. She thinks it's for her money. I..."

It was too much all at once, and as much as Violet tried to be strong and determined, she was crumpling inside. First Agatha, then being a suspect, then Theodophilus. Why did money turn people into such animals?

"Oh, Violet," Lila sighed. "What a mess this is."

Violet just shook her head. How to explain what was happening? She wasn't even sure what *was* happening. What madness was this? They were the fortunate few who didn't have to work and somehow that hadn't become enough for one of them.

Beatrice's eyes were wide as she hung up Violet's earlier dress and straightened her shoes. Violet was one to have a very precisely arranged room, but in her upset, she'd allowed things to get tossed about, and Beatrice put them to rights. Oh! Violet did like that girl.

"Do you believe that someone really is trying to kill your aunt?" Lila asked. She adjusted her hair in the mirror and then said, "What can we do?"

Violet paused and then said, "Yes, I very much believe that

someone is trying to kill Aunt Agatha. The most likely reason is money, which means that the would-be murderer is a member of my family."

Gwennie squeaked at that and Lila scowled at their friend before she turned back to Violet.

"What do we do?"

"Try to get Merry and Algie gossiping. We need to know what is happening with them."

Lila nodded. "That is easy enough, isn't it?"

"Beatrice," Violet turned to the girl and said, "I need you to keep an eye and ear out among the servants. See if you hear anything from them that is strange. I don't expect you to sleuth, and I don't want you at risk."

"Yes, miss."

"But I do want you to see what you can find out by just paying attention. Will you do that?"

"Yes, miss."

"We're lucky to have you," Violet told the maid.

"Thank you, miss," Beatrice said as she left Violet's room.

Vi crossed to the bedroom door as the luncheon gong rang. She slipped into a loose blue dress that reached just past her knees. It was one of her few dresses that had sleeves, as she did enjoy the shape of her shoulders. She sighed as she put it on and then wrapped her new jet beads around her throat finishing off with a pair of matching blue slippers.

Her friends watched her flip through her dresses to find one with sleeves and Lila's gaze was sharp while Gwennie's was wide and worried. Of the two of them, it would be Lila who would fight off an attacker, Violet suddenly thought. She followed that up by hoping that somehow neither of them would come any closer to such a situation than Violet already had. She knew too well that she had been lucky. Beatrice had come at the right moment and she hadn't let Theodophilus scare her off.

"What do you like to do, Beatrice?"

"Oh...um..."

"Do you like working here?"

"I suppose so," Beatrice said slowly.

"We're going to talk about that later. Stay away from Theodophilus. Tell your uncle I said to keep you and the other girls together and away from him."

"Oh, I don't think she has to worry," Lila said as Beatrice paled. "If you think your brother will let someone manhandle you and stay in the same house as you, you are very much mistaken, my dear."

Beatrice brightened at that statement while Gwennie rose.

"We're late, girls." Gwennie stood, tucked a stray hair behind her ear, and leaned into the mirror to adjust her lipstick.

They walked down to the dining room. Aunt Agatha was sitting at the table with the others, but Algernon, Theodophilus, Denny, and Victor were missing.

"Tardiness is incredibly rude," Aunt Agatha said.

"I..." Violet glanced over to her friends and they both shrugged. "I apologize for myself and my friends."

"Sit," Aunt Agatha snapped. "Hargreaves."

Hargreaves entered the dining room and servants followed, placing bowls of fish soup on the table.

"Where is your brother?"

"Ahhh..."

"Don't play games with me, Violet." Agatha's gaze pinned Violet against the chair and she cleared her throat and glanced at Lila, whose gaze was fixed on her soup.

"I believe you would prefer a full explanation in private, ma'am."

Agatha searched Violet's face and then cleared her throat and said, "I didn't expect it to drizzle today. It has been rather colder than last year, I think."

John Davies picked up the conversation thread and mentioned how the hot weather affected the roses. Once John stepped in, low murmuring carried across the table.

Jack was seated next to Violet once again, and he leaned in and asked, "Where is your brother?"

"I don't know," she said, and took a bite of her soup.

He cleared his throat. "I believe you do."

"He is taking care of a problem. His exact whereabouts are unknown."

She could feel Jack's gaze on her and refused to look his way.

"Does it have anything to do with my case? You and your brother need to stay out of it for your own good."

Violet looked at Jack at that statement, unable to hide her anger. "My brother and I will do anything we deem necessary to protect Aunt Agatha; however, he is currently being a protective brother rather than a protective nephew."

Jack's brows rose and Violet scowled at him before she placed her napkin next to her bowl. Luncheon needed to be over soon. Aunt Agatha's cook had outdone himself and the soup was replaced by roasted chicken and potatoes and then finally ices. Violet excused herself as soon as luncheon was over and went looking for her brother, with Lila following along since she'd promised both her husband and Victor to neither be alone or allow Violet to be alone.

"Miss," Beatrice hissed from a doorway and then waved them into a small parlor near the billiards room. "Miss, are you looking for your brother?"

Violet nodded and Beatrice glanced around before she whispered, "He's monitoring Mr. Theodophilus Smythe-Hill, who sent for his bags. My uncle is to drive him to the train station for the afternoon train."

Violet's brows rose and Beatrice said, "Oh, miss. There was quite a row and your brother, well, your brother, he..." She glanced around again and said, "He punched Mr. Smythe-Hill right in jaw. He fell down and then...well...your brother kicked Mr. Smythe-Hill in the stomach while he was on the ground. Mr. Carlyle then lifted him up and did it all again. Mr. Smythe-Hill has quite a large bruise on his jaw; his nose might be broken. And even Mr. Algernon was assaulted. I believe Mr. Algernon may end with a bruise on his jaw and possibly even a black eye!"

"Does he now?" Lila laughed. "This is why your brother will make such a dashing catch when he's ready. The English bulldog is in him."

"He's a lion, not a bulldog." Violet pressed her lips together to hide her grin and then said, "Well...I think we all agree that a form of justice has been served."

"Yes, miss," Beatrice said and then blushed. "I...well...I didn't think Mr. Carlyle would be very happy if you came across him and Mr. Smythe-Hill before he leaves. It wasn't my place to stop you, but..."

"But you did just the right thing, doll," Violet told Beatrice. "You really are one in a million. Now, I had better go apologize to my aunt and explain."

⁓

Violet gave her aunt a very watered-down explanation of what had occurred. She simply explained that Theodophilus insulted her, and Victor felt after such actions Theodophilus should Christmas elsewhere.

Aunt Agatha's mouth twisted up at that, staring at Violet long enough that she shifted around. "I see."

Violet rose to leave and Aunt Agatha said, "Tell your brother I expect the fisticuffs to cease."

Violet paused without looking back at her aunt and said, "Yes, ma'am."

She then made her way to her brother's room. It was empty, but she found the stack of papers which was their newest story. She read it, making notes as she went, clarifying dialogue. Once she was done, she took up the mantle of the storyteller, adding several pages before her brother returned to his room.

"Are you lost, luv?" he asked, flopping down on his bed. "Giles will be quite put out with me; I've ripped my blue-striped suit."

"There are sacrifices when you're the conquering hero," she told him. "Aunt Agatha wants the fisticuffs to cease, but I am happy they occurred."

Victor grinned in reply, and she thought that they'd spent rather enough time on the snake.

"The story is quite good. I like the sinister turn with the butler. Butlers are so often shady creatures, knowing all of our deepest secrets without even trying very hard. It seems quite unfair. Though, Harg-reaves, is, of course, a treasure. His niece possibly surpasses him."

"Blimey bastards butlers are," Victor agreed. "I'm glad to see you've picked up the pen, darling. We're running a bit late for our deadline."

"I can finish it, if you'd like," she told him. "As you may need to ice your knuckles."

"You say that so very blood-thirstily. I believe you like that I gave the snake a good pounding."

"It was a service to womankind. You, sir, are a dashing knight for damsels everywhere."

He grinned at her, but she could still see the banked rage in his gaze.

"I understand you gave Algie a bit of a pounding as well."

"Violet, he owes Theodophilus one thousand pounds."

Violet choked, dropping the pages she'd lifted to hand to Victor. "Oh, no."

"Theodophilus agreed to forgive it only if Algernon successfully introduced you to him and you married the blighter. That idiot Algie thought that the snake could just have you for the asking since you're *past your prime*."

"He never!"

"He did," Victor said, lighting a cigarette and asking, "Pass me the ashtray, luv."

Violet handed him the ashtray and rose to pace. She paused here and there to straighten Victor's hair oil and accoutrements and then adjust the alignment of the port decanter.

"Could he really have offered me up like that?" she murmured after a few minutes of pacing and straightening.

"I got it from Algie's own mouth, luv. After I punched it a time or two. Said he didn't think the snake would manhandle you. Just do the pretty and you'd succumb."

Violet almost growled in reply.

"Denny is seeing the snake all the way onto the train, just to be sure he doesn't try to pull a quick one."

"Vic," Violet sighed, "this puts Algie rather high on the suspect list."

"Didn't really see it in the old boy, myself," Victor said as he lit a second cigarette. "Not sure I do, even now. Algie seemed baffled that Theo grabbed at you the way he did. When I told Algie I'd seen the fingermarks with my own eyes, he still didn't quite believe me. Said he knew Theo could be a blighter, but he'd never seen him hurt a woman."

"Algie never did have a very good imagination. Or the understanding that a person might do something another would never consider."

"He's a blind fool."

Violet sighed and then told Victor, "We're being very neglectful friends to our guests."

"It's why we brought old friends around with us, isn't it? They know we needed them to do what they did today. Stick with you and me when we had *business* to attend to."

"We'll have to have a party when we get home. Or perhaps one in Paris. Something special that they'll enjoy."

"Shall we charter a boat for the Thames? Wine and dancing. Musicians on the water?"

Violet nodded. "We need to write more stories if we keep throwing parties."

"Too right you are, sister. Back to work. No rest for the weary."

Violet laughed at him before she turned back to the typewriter. She worked quickly while Victor read through her notes, adding some of his own. They'd work from their joint notes to create their final version. It would take a few weeks, but their story would be off. If they were very focused, perhaps with a second story as well.

Only finding the would-be killer was the most important thing. But life had to continue didn't it? Aunt Agatha would do her business the next day, even with guests in the house. Lila and Gwennie could be counted on to get Algie or John to play billiards with them and charm life details from the men. Perhaps, later that evening, after a drink or two, they'd discover possible motives for the crime against their aunt.

CHAPTER TWELVE

*V*iolet woke to knocking on her door. When she opened it, she found a flustered Beatrice before her.

"Oh, miss! I'm sorry to wake you. But, miss!"

"Yes, dear?" Violet said, opening the door to let Beatrice into the room. Violet tugged the girl to one of the chairs before the fire and pushed her into it before she pulled off her turban, ran a comb through her hair and then turned to the girl whose gaze was wide and a little terrified. "What is it?"

"It's Mr. Wakefield."

A sudden horror struck Violet and she said, "Jack!"

"Oh. No, miss, it's Mr. James Wakefield. He woke earlier than usual and came down the stairs and...and...someone had greased them! He fell."

"Is he all right?"

"He broke his arm and banged his head well and good. The doctor has been called for, but Mr. Jack said that his father will be all right. But, miss! Mrs. Davies normally gets up earlier on Thursdays to work with the housekeeper on the menu and go over the accounts before the day gets fully started."

"She does, doesn't she? It's another attempt on my aunt's life. I wish she would just retreat to safety. Her stubbornness is going to get her killed."

Beatrice's eyes welled at that and Violet had to leave before she cried along with her. She crossed the hall and banged on her brother's door before she stepped inside.

"Violet! It's the holidays," he moaned. "I was up late again writing."

"There has been another attempt on Aunt Agatha's life," Violet said flatly. "She's all right, but Mr. James Wakefield took a tumble from greased stairs and has a broken arm. The doctor is coming."

Victor cursed and rose, and Violet left him to ring for his man and get dressed. It was time to up their investigation.

"Beatrice, would you please go get coffee for my brother?"

"Yes, of course, miss."

"Be careful, my girl," Violet said. "Whoever is doing this doesn't seem to care if someone else is hurt. Mr. Wakefield has nearly died twice in defense of my aunt."

Beatrice's gaze was worried as she nodded several times. "Yes, miss. Of course, miss. Please be careful as well. I think...well...I think you are at rather more risk than a housemaid."

Violet dressed in a hurry even though she knew that there was nothing she could do at the moment. When she reached the breakfast room, it was empty. She asked Hargreaves and he said, "Miss Meredith ate and has, I believe, gone to the library. Mr. Algernon has yet to appear. Mr. Jack Wakefield is with his father. Mr. John has eaten and taken his car into town to 'lighten the load for the household.'"

Violet's brows rose and she said, "Have you sent in coffee or breakfast to the Misters Wakefield?"

Hargreaves shook his head and she said, "Perhaps you'd better."

He nodded and disappeared into the kitchens. A few moments later while Violet sat at the table with a cup of tea, there was a ruckus at the front door. She rose and went to it, guessing the household was too busy to attend the door when no one was expected. She opened it and stepped back in surprise at the sight of her Uncle Kingsley.

He was a corpulent fellow with a good half of his hair gone and the rest on retreat. His chins waggled at the sight of her answering the door and his face was ruddy with either the cold or anger. She tried smiling at him to no avail.

"Whatever are you opening doors for, gel? Where is Hargreaves? I've come in response to my fool boy who can't handle matters on his own."

"Hargreaves is attending to a household emergency," Violet replied, gesturing for her uncle to enter.

Uncle Kingsley barged through the door, dropping his coat, hat, and gloves on a chair and blustering, "I am unsurprised to find Agatha's house in a uproar. She seems to be losing her wits. I suppose you're here for the bullion? Well it won't do. Won't do at all. That money should go to my generation."

Violet didn't bother to answer that statement. "Aunt Agatha has yet to come downstairs, I believe. There is breakfast."

Uncle Kingsley stomped into the breakfast room, gaze darting about, and then he rang the bell wildly. "No surprise my boy isn't down here. Always was a lazy good-for-nothing."

Violet considered retreating but decided against it. She took a seat and returned to her tea when the doorbell rang again. This time she let in the doctor, leading him up to Mr. Wakefield's room, past a servant who was scrubbing the stairs.

"There seems to have been some grease on the stairs," Violet told him when they passed the girl. "It caused Mr. James Wakefield's accident."

"Did it now?" Doctor Cumming replied. He was bright enough to know there was more to the story and wise enough to not ask more questions.

To say Jack Wakefield was infuriated wasn't clear enough. The door opened, his furious gaze seemed to set her on fire, and she stepped back for Dr. Cumming to enter the room. Violet didn't even attempt to stay. She just asked, "Do you need anything else?"

"We've had quite enough," Jack snapped.

Violet flinched and an expression of regret passed over his face. His father called his name and Jack said, "Forgive me." He then shut the door in her face. Violet shrugged, debated her options, and returned to the breakfast room.

She set aside her cold tea and made a fresh cup, this time taking a plate of fruit, tomatoes, and eggs.

Uncle Kingsley had a loaded plate, a large cup of tea, and a newspaper. He tossed the paper to the side and demanded, "What the dickens is happening, gel?"

Violet sat quietly, desperately wishing for her brother, when a huge crash came from the east wing.

"Oh dear," Violet said as Uncle Kingsley cursed. "I believe that might be the coffee tray we sent up."

"What in the bloody hell is happening here?" Uncle Kingsley demanded.

"There has been an accident. I believe Mr. Jack Wakefield may have just lost his temper on the silver."

"And who the dickens is this ill-tempered Wakefield?" Uncle Kingsley yelled.

Violet did not miss the irony as she calmly said, "Mr. James and Mr. Jack Wakefield are two of Aunt Agatha's guests for the holidays."

"And they believe it is acceptable to throw about her silver? Time to send the woman off to bedlam before madness overcomes us all."

Violet's gaze narrowed on her uncle and she snapped, "Mr. James Wakefield nearly lost his life in an accident this morning. The ire Mr. Jack Wakefield feels is surely justifiable given the near-loss of his father's life."

"I hardly think it appropriate to act in such a manner," Uncle Kingsley yelled. "Now where is my son? I sent the maid for him quite a while ago."

"Uncle Kingsley," Violet snapped, "You have not been here for twenty minutes. You have spent the entirety of that time yelling and insulting my aunt in her own home. I hardly think you are in the position to cast aspersions on the behavior of Aunt Agatha's guests when your own behavior is reprehensible."

"Reprehensible? Who do you think you are, gel? I am your elder."

"And," Violet hissed, "on a normal day I would treat you with the respect your age deserves. However, I will not stand by and watch you insult my aunt and the behavior of her guests when you have no reference point for why they are behaving as they are."

"I will be speaking to your father," he snarled, "and your aunt."

"Please do," she replied calmly.

The door of the breakfast room opened and both Victor and Algernon entered.

"Where is Hargreaves?" shouted Uncle Kingsley.

"There has been an accident, Father," Algie said. "Of course he's seeing to the needy."

"The old fellow who fell down the stairs and then his son had a tantrum? I suppose someone has to deal with them. I was under the impression this was a full-grown man we were dealing with. Is he damaged from the war?"

"Ah..." Victor said. "Well..."

"I think I'll just go find Meredith," Violet said brightly. "So nice to see you, Uncle."

"And where is Agatha? Sending threatening letters and demanding a body's presence during the holidays. If I'd wanted to come see the old gel during the holidays, I'd bloody well have made it known, wouldn't I?"

"Ah..." Victor replied, clearing his throat. Violet winked at him as she shut the door, ignoring the supplicating look on his face.

Violet ran up the stairs to her rooms, knocking on Gwennie's door and warning her to stay away from the breakfast room and to save Lila and Denny as well.

"What is happening?" Gwennie asked when Lila opened the door to the bedroom she and Denny shared.

"There has been another attempt on Aunt Agatha," Violet sighed. "Mr. James Wakefield was the victim. He'll be all right, I understand, but the doctor is with him. My uncle has arrived, and he's in a rage. It's just safer, darlings, to eat toast in your room. I'll send some up, shall I? Then perhaps you all will want to visit the town today or play a few rounds of billiards. I'm so sorry things are dire. This was not at all what I imagined when we invited you."

"Not to worry, darling," Lila said while Gwennie squeaked in shock. "We will be fine. How can we help?"

"Perhaps the town trip? See if you can find John Davies? He left as soon as they found Mr. Wakefield to get out of the way. See what you can find out about him?"

Gwennie nodded a little too enthusiastically, and Violet realized her friend may just have developed some puppy love for her cousin-by-marriage.

Lila's lush lips twitched at the expression on Gwennie's face and she said, "Yes, I think we'd better."

Gwennie blushed furiously and disappeared into her room as Lila asked low, "Darling, are you all right?"

"I lost my temper with my uncle," Violet confessed. "I am sure Aunt Agatha will be hearing about it shortly. He came in a rage and just said the most horrible things, and I...I...just snapped."

Lila smirked and then said, "Well, darling, I'm sure you were justified."

"Perhaps, but it is so hard to prove when he's my father's age and I called him to repentance." Violet could feel the heat on her cheeks. "I am ashamed of myself. I shouldn't have lost control."

"You will apologize prettily, bat your lovely lashes, and blame your womanly weakness. He won't be able to avoid accepting your apology. That's what comes from being such a lovely thing."

Violet scowled. She would need several drinks before she could muster up the strength of will for such a lie.

"Don't forget to flatter him outrageously, darling," Lila trilled.

Bloody hell, Violet thought as she realized she would have to do just that. Lila's mocking laughter chased Violet down the stairs and into the kitchens where she requested trays sent to her friends and apologized for the extra work.

The cook nodded sharply, clearly frustrated, and Violet paused to flatter her as well before escaping to see Meredith in the library.

CHAPTER THIRTEEN

"*M*eredith," Violet called. "Hello, dear. Uncle Kingsley has arrived with his blood up, and I thought I might hide with you."

"Left your friends to it, did you?"

"I've warned them off. I believe they may spend the day in town as Uncle Kingsley came through the door with the devil in his eye," Violet laughed. "My friends are bright young things after all. They don't linger for the dull family fighting. We haven't had a chance for a good chat yet, have we? You're near Chigwell these days, aren't you? Near your parents?"

"Indeed no, though I was coming from there when we met on the train," Meredith said sourly. She sniffed and closed her book, giving Violet a look that said she was very much interrupting.

Violet smiled brightly and ignored Meredith's silent order to vacate. "Where are you then, dear?"

"About two hours from here, actually," Meredith said, sniffing once again. "My sister pled for assistance and I arrived forthwith. Family should help each other after all. Support in one's time of need."

Violet grinned brightly and winced inside. Assistance? More like an unpaid servant. If Violet knew anything about Gertrude, and Violet knew very little, she knew that Gertrude was cheap, sour, and inclined to order about anyone weaker than herself. The few times they had met had not left either cousin pleased with the other.

"Doesn't she have children these days?"

"Five in four years," Meredith said. "She had twins as well. Twins are an affliction on a family. Not that I intend to offend you and Victor, but I have to speak the truth."

Violet gaily laughed and said, "Oh, none taken, darling. Believe me, that is not the first time someone has made such a statement to Victor or myself. We were rather a handful when we were children, weren't we?"

Meredith sharply nodded and then she rose to ring the bell. When Beatrice arrived in the library moments later, it was evident that she'd been cleaning nearby. There was a bit of dust on her cheek and she was red-faced with exertion.

"Mrs. Halvert? Miss Violet?"

"Technically speaking, Violet should be called Lady," Meredith told Beatrice, who flushed brilliantly.

"I don't use my title," Violet countered. "Not really. Miss is simply perfect, dear Beatrice."

"Tea, please," Meredith demanded. "Sandwiches or biscuits or toast. Something to nibble."

"Yes, ma'am," Beatrice said, disappearing quickly.

Meredith scowled after her and said, "She's too pretty to be a servant. And rather too bright-eyed. No doubt she listens at doors."

Violet's expression didn't change, but she said, "I quite like her. She's...stalwart."

"Stalwart? A very odd term to be using for some country house-maid who probably spends each afternoon flirting with the footman and dreaming over the young men of the house, telling herself if they only knew her they could love her despite the difference in class."

Violet had to keep her mouth shut and remind herself that she was there for details of Meredith's life. As much as Violet would like to imagine otherwise, each of the attempts on Aunt Agatha's life could easily have been done by a woman as a man. Her current preference for murderer was Algernon. Or John Davies. She didn't really care one way or the other about the blank slate that was John Davies, and Algernon had tried to use her to pay his gambling debts.

Meredith, on the other hand, had a rather hard time of it for the entirety of her life, and Violet wanted to wrap the sour old thing up in a bit of loving. Maybe from a distance. See Meredith in some remote seaside cottage where it would be quite inconvenient to visit but where she might be happy.

"What do you think of the village where your sister lives? Are there a lot of people there?"

"It is a typical English village. The lending library is lacking, the gossip between the housewives is without end, and there are more widows than there should be. Gertrude has quite a time of it with the way some of the country housewives treat her. They don't seem to realize how well connected she is and don't treat her with the respect she deserves."

Violet winced for Meredith and Gertrude. They were living in the old days when their grandmothers could lord it over their neighbors because a cousin had been the third wife to an earl. Of all the ridiculous things. If the war had taught them anything, hadn't it taught them that birth didn't make one better or worse than another? After months and years in the trenches with the nobility working side by side the lower classes, dying together, surely they could see that there was nothing particularly special about being the child of an earl? Violet didn't feel special as compared to Meredith. Simply more fortunate in her parentage. That didn't even have to do with her father being an earl. Uncle Cecil was undesirable even if he had been the earl.

Violet might disappoint her father and stepmother, but they loved her and would never see her working for a married sister.

She gently said, "I can't even imagine how hard it must be for you, Meredith. Losing your husband as you did."

"Yes, well. Better to have loved and lost than to have never loved at all." Her fixed gaze told Violet exactly who would never love at all and she found herself biting back a sharp retort once again.

Violet reminded herself that Meredith had been very unfortunate and counted herself blessed to have avoided the same pain, when Beatrice opened the door, interrupting the awkward conversation by setting out the tea things.

"Did you want to pour, luv? Or shall I?"

Meredith scowled as she poured. "Have you read anything enriching lately? I've been pursing *A Treatise on Domestic Economy*. We are so wasteful as a people. Frittering money away on the most useless of things and throwing out what could be used wisely."

Violet smiled brightly despite being unqualified to say a single nice thing about an entire *treatise* on penny pinching. She confessed, "I'm afraid I have not read one enriching or educational thing since Oxford, darling. I am rather addicted to French novels, pulp magazines, and the occasional scandalous play."

"Well, I am unsurprised. You always were flighty."

Violet smiled at that. She had been rather flighty as a child. She did, in fact, relish being flighty as an adult. She might have lied about her intellectual pursuits, but she'd be damned if she got pulled into a conversation about domestic economy. If she had been honest, she read the financial papers and reports from Aunt Agatha's companies as well as essays about women's rights, but Violet didn't want to hear Meredith's inevitable lecture about such things, and to be honest with herself, she much preferred the scandalous French novels. Let alone, her fierce love for the Tarzan stories of Edgar Rice Burroughs.

Aunt Agatha had a shipping company that went between London and New York, and Violet had commissioned the captain to get her the American novels by Edgar Rice Burroughs every time he went along with anything that fell into the same line. He was good enough to acquire the American pulp magazines as well. Though, she let Victor take credit for ownership should anyone notice them on their shelves.

"Victor and I were thinking of going to Paris after our visit with Aunt Agatha. Would you like to come with us? We're staying with a friend and the cost will be very minimal."

Meredith seemed almost shocked for a moment, her mouth agape. Violet rather felt the same. The invitation had escaped her before she'd fully thought it through.

"It should be dismal weather and a terrible crossing, but I think that, in general, we'll have a rather fine time. French chefs are so much better than British ones, don't you know?"

"My sister needs me," Meredith said, twisting her mouth sourly and scowling at the affront of Violet's invitation.

"Oh, darling. A visit to Paris is good for the soul."

"I hardly think so. No doubt you'll be drinking and dancing with little consideration of the finer morals or elevating yourself."

And, with that, Violet decided to not push the matter. "No doubt you're right, darling. We do enjoy our grasshoppers and gin rickeys. Let alone dancing. A little jazz music, a little of the city by starlight. Perhaps a jaunt down to the vineyards to find something delicious to add to the cellars."

Meredith scowled as she said, "Foolish drinks with foolish names for foolish minds."

"Fun drinks with fun names for fun times. Foolish minds, I'll give you." Violet took a fortifying drink of her tea and grabbed a biscuit. A little shortbread dunked in her tea just to watch Meredith's mouth twist up into a scowl.

Yes, Violet was definitely going to be consigned to hell for tormenting her cousin, but her already weak better nature failed her entirely.

CHAPTER FOURTEEN

"What did you find out?" Victor asked, as Violet joined her brother, Denny, Lila, and Gwennie in Victor's room that evening. Lila had taken the chair near the fire and was reading their story, while Denny and Victor were smoking near the window. Gwennie sat across from Lila, book in her lap, looking up with a curious gaze. "Any changes for good ole Merry?"

"She is as sour as she ever was. We were cruel to give her that name, but Victor—" Violet shook her head and started her pacing. She stopped to cover the typewriter and straighten their paper stack and then continued. "She got manipulated into moving in with Gertrude, who has a passel of terrible children."

"Oh, no," Lila said. "It's the nightmare of every widow and spinster."

"It's worse than you know," Violet declared. "Gertrude has had five children in four years including twins." Violet paused dramatically and added, "Who—like all twins—are an affliction on their family."

Victor snorted and then said, "Well, Merry's not wrong there."

"I do feel sorry for her. I even invited her to Paris—"

A chorus of, "Oh, nos!" and, "You didn'ts!" filled the air and Violet held up her hand.

"Not to worry, my loves, she has no interest in foolish drinks with foolish people who foolishly fritter their time without thought of higher things."

"Thank God!" Victor muttered and then said, "Don't be kind again, sister mine."

"I'll endeavor to bring my inner shrew to the forefront for the rest of our stay here."

Lila laughed while Gwennie shuddered. "I'm sorry, Vi. But your cousins are simply awful."

"Oh darling, we know," Violet told Gwennie. "It was why we pled so fervently for you to rally round. The thing is, my loves, Meredith's life *has* changed. And she's closer than we thought. Gertrude lives with her husband in Shelby which is only two hours from here. It would have been possible for Meredith to commit all of the crimes herself whereas Algie would have had to hire someone to help."

"And," Victor added, "with Uncle Kingsley appearing at the threat of really being left out of the will, he has to be added to the suspect list."

"Has your uncle had any material changes lately? Something that might drive him to murder for money?" Denny asked. He put out his cigarette and crossed to his wife, settling his hand on her shoulder for a moment and squeezing.

Victor shrugged and Violet echoed it. It wasn't as though they were close with Uncle Kingsley. Perhaps they were invited to a dinner a year, if that.

"How is Mr. James, Victor?"

"Ran into Jack. He said his father is drugged up and plastered up, but will be fine. He had quite the rage in his gaze though. I wouldn't want to cross Jack Wakefield for all the money in the Bank of London."

"Mmmm," Violet agreed. The enraged Jack had been somewhat terrifying, but she was so glad to hear that his father would be all right. The memory of her sudden pain that morning, when she'd thought that *Jack* had been the one hurt, returned. What was this between them? She was his suspect. He was an investigator. A would-be murderer was on the loose, and her heart was skipping a beat nearly every time they touched.

"And has anyone seen Aunt Agatha?"

"She kept to her rooms today," Victor said. "Despite the bellows of Uncle Kingsley."

"A brilliant woman, your aunt," Lila laughed. "We found your Mr. Davies in town. Spent much of the day with him. Gwennie made calf eyes at him, and he seemed intrigued with her charming smile. We learned that he lives in Leeds, works with his father, is a bachelor, and has always enjoyed Aunt Agatha's *spice*."

"So you learned nothing to rule him out?"

"Only that he has the good taste to admire our Gwennie's fine eyes."

Gwennie blushed and said, "Oh, stop it!"

"Well," Victor said, "this holiday will be one to remember if we survive it."

"Now you stop it, brother," Violet ordered. She rose and asked, "Shall we play a game of billiards?"

"No," Victor said, "*we* will. Darling, you check on Aunt Agatha and make sure she's all right."

Violet nodded and left her brother's rooms. She walked to Aunt Agatha's bedroom with her hand firmly on the rail of the stairs. Violet had never noted how steep they were. It infuriated her that what had once been a beautiful staircase with an eye to the beauty of detailing was suddenly something to be feared.

When she went to knock on Aunt Agatha's door, Jack Wakefield stepped out of his father's room.

"Oh," she said lamely and then followed up with, "How is your father?"

"He'll be fine," Jack snapped and then closed his eyes, seeming to take himself in hand before he said, "Forgive me. I shouldn't have spoken to you like that. Now or earlier today. May I have a few moments of your time?"

Violet nodded, and Jack led her down the hallway a bit. "This has got to stop."

"I agree."

"I need you to tell me why your brother assaulted Theodophilus Smythe-Hill and Algernon."

Violet paused and then decided that lying or evading questions from the man who was trying to protect her aunt wasn't a choice she could make. She glanced around, noted a scullery maid and said, "Perhaps we can walk some?"

Jack held out his arm, and she slowly took it. "It starts with Algernon. He has something of a sordid history of throwing his friends my way with too much information about my potential inheritances."

Jack seemed to almost growl in the back of his throat though his face didn't change. He took a rather tight grip on her arm as they walked down the stairs and then he led her to the back of the house where the orangery would be both warm and private.

"He seems to have lost rather a lot of money to the snake, Theodophilus."

"Has he?" Jack asked silkily.

Violet knew he'd see the motive in that statement and as much as she regretted that for Algie, Aunt Agatha was higher on Violet's list of concerns than her cousin's money troubles.

"They agreed between themselves that if Theodophilus married me after being introduced by Algie that the debt would be forgiven."

Violet blushed as Jack stopped. He dropped her hand and clenched his fist, so Violet took a seat on one of the stone benches, reaching down to trail her fingers over the plants that were growing nearby.

"My father will settle enough on me that—with the money from my mother and grandfather—it would make it unnecessary to struggle or work. However, I don't believe that the snake wished for the money so much as the connection to my father. He is an earl, after all. It doesn't mean all that much to me, but the snake thinks rather differently about the old connections. When you add in Aunt Agatha's business connections and Uncle Kingsley and his friends, I suppose my connections are worth rather more than my semi-respectable inheritance."

Jack dropped down onto the bench across the path from her and asked, "So your brother assaulted him for that? It seems rather a strong reaction."

Violet didn't want to relive the fear she'd felt as the snake manhandled her, but she had determined to be honest with Jack and help him find who was trying to hurt Aunt Agatha. Violet dropped her gaze to the ground and said, "Well. No. The snake caught me alone and...well... he manhandled me some. I was...well, I was afraid. If Hargreaves's niece, Beatrice, hadn't come along at just the right moment, I'm not sure what would have happened. I told Victor and he shrugged off his affable nature, gathered Denny up, and taught both the snake and Algie a lesson."

Jack's hands were grasping the stone bench so tightly that his fingers had turned white. Violet felt a moment of concern, but as her gaze flicked over his face, she realized she was entirely safe with him. This was an honorable man. The kind you called on when you were being threatened as Aunt Agatha had. This was the man who went to war and protected his country. No doubt he'd had some image of ideal England that he had been fighting for, but fight he did. It didn't matter really why he'd fought or why he was here now. She was sure she was safe with him and that flash of trepidation died.

"That makes Algernon a much more interesting suspect than he was a few minutes ago. I wish you had told me earlier."

"There's more," Violet said, explaining the change in Meredith's circumstances. Jack seemed far less inclined to find Meredith's situation suspicious. Violet supposed it seemed like the fate of many a woman after the war with so many men lost, but she wasn't sure she agreed that it was so unremarkable. No woman wanted the life Meredith was leading. Having loved and lost and then being imprisoned in an unloving sibling's home. Even if Meredith was fond of the children, they weren't hers, were they? Her fate was to be powerless just as women were starting to really find a foothold in crafting their own lives.

Violet, herself, was an example of this. Her mother would never have been able to live in the city with an indulgent brother, writing stories on the side, and spending her evenings dating whom she chose. She was as likely to dance with a poor artist as a son of a peer, and neither were more appealing than the other. Even this attraction she felt for Jack would have been impossible in her mother and grand-mother's day. In these modern times, anything was possible.

Violet refused to let Jack go until she pointed out that Uncle Kingsley had arrived. It didn't make him more suspicious than any of the rest, but he'd responded to the threat, which told Violet that Uncle Kingsley expected to inherit from his aunt. Maybe for himself. Maybe for his children. Either way, he had an eye on Aunt Agatha's money.

"I told you what I found out," Violet said to Jack. She could feel his gaze on her almost as though he were touching her. First her collar-bone, then her cheek, then the curve of her lips. "Tell me what you have found."

"No," Jack said, flatly. "It's dangerous. This person is trying to *kill* your aunt. I won't put you in the line of fire as well."

Violet hesitated and then said, "I can't make you tell me. But you are spiting yourself. I may well be able to provide context that even Aunt Agatha cannot. She doesn't know all the secrets of myself and my cousins. We're the main suspects, aren't we?"

"You are a suspect," Jack told her honestly. "You all are. I haven't been able to entirely rule anyone out."

"Then ask me your questions. Tell me what you know. Let me help."

"If you are the criminal," Jack said gently. "Or your brother, your context could lead me astray."

"Better astray but moving forward than blindly treading water," Violet shot back. "I won't deny that I hate being a suspect. I hate that Aunt Agatha is concerned that I might be trying to hurt her. That you think I might have caused your father's accident. That anyone could believe my focus is so on money that I've forgotten my soul, but I swear to you I have not."

"And your brother? Do you think I don't see how he is in the fore-front of your heart and mind? You would lie for him."

"We shared a womb! I know him better than I know myself. I don't *have* to lie for him."

"Or you think you know him and are wrong," Jack said almost gently. "I checked out your marriage proposal. I checked out that

Tomas St. Marks is really as rich as gossip says. I believe that you have a much easier way to get money. That doesn't extend to your brother."

"Of course it does!" Violet said. "If I married Tomas, Victor's very best friend, do you think that Victor wouldn't live in our household? Do you think Victor doesn't wish I loved Tomas as he deserves to be loved? He does. He does because it would put the two of them together. They're brothers in their hearts. Victor would live with us. He'd lose the expense of a household, and he wouldn't need more money."

"And when he wants to marry?"

Violet took in a slow breath and then said, "Victor is not a monster. He loves Agatha as much as I do."

"I'd love to believe in him as fiercely as you do, Violet." His hand twitched. Perhaps he wanted to reach towards her, but instead, he re-grasped the bench. "I won't risk your aunt on sentiment."

"All I am saying is that if you ask me questions about what you've learned, I might be able to help. Fine! Investigate us! Slap us on your suspect list. We're on mine. But you'll find, in the end, that it wasn't Victor or myself. Let me help. Please. By Jove, if I'm not lying to you, Aunt Agatha is the closest thing I've had to a mother since I lost my own. Please, let me help. Please."

Jack's penetrating gaze flicked over her and then he said, "Your Uncle Kingsley has taken some rather spectacular losses."

Violet leaned back, shocked to her bones.

"No doubt the reason Algernon offered you up was because his father was unable to rescue him this time from his idiocy. It turns out this isn't the first time that Algernon has lost money like this."

Violet leaned back, thinking over what she knew of Uncle Kingsley, Algernon, and...she hated to say it...Victor. Finally she told Jack, "Victor must have known that."

"Why do you say that?"

"A few months ago, Algernon went from annoying cousin to almost seeming to flirt with me. I told Victor about it, and it stopped. I wouldn't be surprised if he found out about the money. Algie doesn't know me well enough to understand I won't be married for whatever money I have. Algie wants to believe I'm desperate to be married despite the rumors of Tomas."

"Do you love Tomas?" Jack asked Violet, and suddenly it didn't seem like a question from an investigator. It felt rather like a question from a man to a woman. A man who might have noticed her eyes or her wit. A man who might see something in her. Something intriguing? Something possibly worth loving?

Her breath hitched, just a little, and she met his gaze. She told him, very clearly, "Tomas is my brother's best friend. He has problems from the war. He feels secure with me. As for me, he has always made me feel safe and loved."

Jack's jaw tightened, but his face was impassive beyond that.

"It's just that I don't love him that way. I feel the same towards Tomas as I do towards Victor. I don't want to marry Tomas. I want him to marry someone who loves him desperately and then be chums with her."

CHAPTER FIFTEEN

"*B*ack to Kingsley," Jack said. "What else do you know?"

"How much did he lose?"

Jack paused and then said, "Everything he has and more."

"Oh, Uncle Kingsley," Violet whispered. What would he do? Algernon could get a job and use his connections to see to himself. But Uncle Kingsley was a bit old to start a career and far too proud. He had children in the schoolroom and a wife to support. What a terrible mess! Why did people invest beyond their means? Why would anyone risk everything? Aunt Agatha had taught Violet time and again about proceeding with caution. About building a fortune slowly and with steady steps.

It was those same principles that had helped Violet and Victor increase their own income. Careful investing, careful purchases, careful, deliberate risks that wouldn't handicap them.

"Did he ask Aunt Agatha to rescue him?"

"It is my understanding that he suggested to her that she join the investment, and she advised him strenuously against it. He's since asked her for help, but she refuses to throw good money after bad."

Violet could well imagine it. Uncle Kingsley had often acted as though Aunt Agatha's success was a series of fortunate happenstances that had given her an unjustified sense of understanding business. Violet knew he was wrong about Agatha, but no one could convince Kingsley—a man—that his aunt might just be smarter in business than he was. Violet had heard him prose on, more than once, about the weakness of women's minds, about their lack of capacity for mathematics and the sciences. About the way their minds were easily persuaded into the gothic and supernatural.

Violet was used as an example far too often because of her love of novels. Whereas Victor, who loved all the same novels, was never held up. He was a man who enjoyed a little fluff here and there. As though Violet could believe the great apes of Africa would raise a baby and Victor would recognize it as a fairy story. Of course, Violet recognized her novels as stories, but it didn't matter. She was the fool and Victor was never reprimanded.

Violet gritted her teeth and leapt off her bench to pace in front of Jack. She muttered under her breath about the stupidity of men who assumed they were so wise and experienced because of a difference in plumbing. Her steps were quick and sharp and her words were barely audible. It seemed, from the smile on Jack's face, that he caught too many of them. In her fury, she didn't care.

"He's here to keep himself in the will or get himself into it," she stated with surety. "He's got to be desperate for the money."

"Do you think he's not in it?"

Violet considered for a few minutes as she paced, her slippers clicking against the stone of the pathways before she said, "I doubt it. Aunt Agatha has never appreciated the way Kingsley has treated her. He always has this attitude that her fortune is a lucky accident and she should turn the control of it to him before she loses it all. She's not a cypher despite his desire that she would be. Nor is Aunt Agatha the type of woman, with an excess of heirs, to give money to one who spent his life treating her as a fool."

Jack nodded and then said, "What about Algernon? What would he do if he realized his inheritance from his father was gone?"

Violet's steps continued. She had always been a pacer. Someone who moved while she thought. In the face of a potential murder, it was even worse.

"I don't know. Aunt Agatha is fond of him, I think. When we were children, Algie, Merry, Vic, and I spent a lot of time with Aunt Agatha. John Davies on occasion as well. I don't know that she favored any of us over the others. I really did think she'd leave her money to a hospital or a school. But if she's determined to comply with her husband's wishes to build a fortune as a gift for those she loves, then I would think the five of us would be the most likely heirs."

"Do you think she'll give it all to one?"

"Why would she do that?" Violet asked, genuinely shocked. "Just so one of us could be very blessed and the rest of us would look on in envy? That will ruin relationships. I don't think so. Maybe for John since he was related to Henry. But Aunt Agatha doesn't err on the side of the men like so many do. Merry and I are as likely to inherit as Vic and Algie."

"Do you believe your cousin Algie would murder his aunt once he realized the fortune of his father was gone, he was in debt, and no one would save him?"

Violet hesitated and then admitted, "He's thoughtless. I...maybe? But perhaps not. I could more see Theo killing Agatha to get the money back from Algie. Algie himself? I think he might just make grand promises about her imminent death even though he didn't have any reason to actually believe she is at death's door."

"So who do you think is the would-be killer?"

Violet bit her lip and then admitted, "I...wish I could say I knew. I wish I had some reason to believe it was someone else. Anyone else. Of my family? I haven't a clue."

Jack made a note in a notebook she hadn't even noticed and then he asked, "What would Agatha do if she realized Algie has a gambling problem?"

Violet hadn't thought about that. Agatha didn't suffer fools and Violet could almost hear her say, 'I'll be damned if I spend a lifetime building an income and let him fritter it away.'

Now that she thought about it, how often had Aunt Agatha tried to teach them about investing? About curating your fortune? About carefully looking into where you might put your money? Violet would gamble her own money that neither Merry or Algie had ever listened to Agatha. Even Victor had only learned those things because he loved Agatha, not because he wanted to spend his time that way. He wasn't a man for business.

If Agatha didn't trust them with the money she'd built, just how would she leave it to them?

"I don't know," Violet said. "Does she not know? You make it seem like this has been a problem for a while for Algie. I wouldn't be surprised if she is well aware of his issues. But, as far as the inheritance? I doubt she'd just hand him money that he could lose in months when it took her years to build it. Only..."

"Only?"

"Only there are ways around that, aren't there? She could leave him a trust he couldn't access the principal of? She'd probably do that for Merry, to be honest. Aunt Agatha was not at all pleased when she realized that the money Meredith received from Grandfather was gone before her husband had even died."

Jack winced and Violet nodded. "Her husband got control of it when they wed, and when he died, she was left with nothing. Victor and I wondered, more than once, if her husband had married her for that very reason and then scolded ourselves for thinking it."

Jack leaned back and he asked, "What about you and Victor?"

A part of Violet wanted to lie. She knew that Aunt Agatha was not displeased with how they'd treated their own money. Violet had asked for Agatha's advice on more than one investment that Violet had pursued. Violet had received and followed suggestions that Agatha had sent.

"I think, of the five of us, that Agatha might trust Victor and myself with the money without restriction."

"Why you?"

Violet spent a few minutes describing how Agatha had tried to teach all of them about investing and growing a fortune. About how Violet read and responded to reports that Agatha sent. "Looking back, Aunt Agatha has been training us since we were children. If she really built her fortune for us, for the five of us, she's been trying to prepare us to protect it."

"And you and Victor learned when the others didn't?"

"Victor and I don't talk about money with our family. But we've been investing according to Aunt Agatha's suggestions as long as we've been able to. We've increased our own allowance because of it."

"Have you now?" Jack looked suddenly intrigued.

"We aren't on track to be as rich as Agatha. Not at any point. We enjoy spending money too much. But, we're doing fine all the same. Everyone is so concerned about when Victor might have to support a wife, but give us five more years of steady increases, and he will be able to have a family without ever needing to punch the workplace clock."

"You realize that this provides a motive. If you had realized that such a fortune could be yours, well...money has turned more than one head."

"I realize that," Violet said simply. "I can't make you believe that we're happy with our lives as they are. And I realize that you can hear me speak for Victor and assume I don't know what I'm talking about, but that's not the case. You'll find the would-be killer, right? You'll save Aunt Agatha, and then—perhaps—you can believe me."

"It isn't that I wouldn't like to believe you now," Jack said gently, almost fervently. He stood, but he didn't step closer. She could feel his gaze like a brand on her skin, on her face. He was making her feel small again, only somehow safer than she'd ever been. "I won't risk your aunt on what I'd like to believe. Unfortunately, money provides rather a good motive for all of you to kill her. There's no evidence over who could have made any of the attempts. They were failures, but well thought out beyond failing. Each of you are smart enough to have done each of them. If she split her money, all of you would benefit from one murderous action."

"I don't consider losing my aunt as benefiting, but I see what you mean."

Jack nodded and offered Violet his arm. They left the orangery and made their way back to the main part of the house. The sound of shouting stopped them both.

"So you'll just leave them to suffer?"

The screaming was coming from the other side of Aunt Agatha's office door. Her reply was far lower, and they couldn't hear it, but Violet whispered to Jack, "That's Uncle Kingsley."

The next round of shouting didn't make it through the thick doors beyond the sound of fury.

"He might be asking for help again."

Violet nodded and winced as Uncle Kingsley's shouting escalated. "You are an accident of fate. Nothing more. Would that we were all as lucky as you and your golden touch."

Violet could imagine the sneer on her uncle's face. The door across from the office cracked. Lila peeked out of the billiards room, saw Jack, and stepped back. She left the door open to better hear. Violet angled away from the open door to avoid drawing attention to her friends.

The shouting increased in intensity until only occasional insults could be heard. "Selfish...cruel...no regard for family...."

Violet winced with each accusation, feeling for her aunt. The woman had loved Violet from the day Mama had asked Aunt Agatha to look after them. She'd spent the last two decades seeing to their education and love.

CHAPTER SIXTEEN

*V*iolet entered Aunt Agatha's office with trepidation and a tea tray. Her aunt looked up from her desk slowly, brows raised.

"I thought you might trust me to give you a drink again."

Her aunt's snort told her that she didn't find the statement any more humorous than Violet did, but when Violet poured two cups of tea, her aunt took one.

"What are you working on?" Violet poured cream into her tea and added sugar without thought until she realized she'd added far too much. Rather than call for another cup, she decided to reap what she'd sowed and choked down the first sip.

"Some ideas," Agatha said vaguely. She took a sip of her own tea and then asked, "Why don't you have a maid?"

"I can't afford one who will stay," Violet admitted. "You have to out pay the factories in London for a girl to be willing to press your clothes and mend your stockings. Victor has Giles, who manages our rooms, and we have a daily who comes in to help. I, can you believe it, mend my own stockings."

"Shocking," Aunt Agatha laughed. Her eyes crinkled with humor and they flashed on Violet's face. If the weight of a potential murder weren't pressing against them, they'd have had a conversation like this a half dozen times over since Violet had arrived. Instead this awful distance divided them.

She sat on the other side of a massive desk facing the room. Large windows were behind her. Light came through, but there were heavy curtains, thick and lush to keep out of the cold if she wished. It was rare, however, for Aunt Agatha to shut out the light. She'd rather have the view and a need of a shawl.

"Did you read my report about the Morris automobile company?" Agatha asked, her fingers tangled over her stomach.

Violet rose and started to arrange the papers on Agatha's desk. There was a stack of unopened mail, and she opened it for her. Messes, like the one on Agatha's desk, made Violet's fingers itch. Violet took Agatha's letter opener and opened the letters, stacked them with their envelopes and set them for Aunt Agatha to go through.

As she worked, Meredith opened the door, saw them and said, "Oh." Her gaze flicked over the two of them.

"Hello, dear," Agatha said, "I am happy to see you, but I was wanting to speak to each of you individually today. I'll send for you soon, all right?"

Meredith did not look pleased when she nodded and left. Agatha turned back to Violet and asked, "Now where were we? Did you read that report I sent?"

Violet paused, gathered her thoughts back from Meredith and said, "I did read it."

"And what did you think?"

"I think you've invested in the Rolls-Royce already. Would you be competing against yourself?"

"What do you think?" Agatha asked, one brow raised. There was no doubt that Violet was being quizzed by Agatha. Just what was she looking for? General assurance that Violet didn't ignore her aunt or something more? Could whoever was attempting to kill Aunt Agatha have something to do with the shares in those companies?

"I think that both companies look as though they are doing well," Violet admitted. "There seems to be room enough in Britain to create automobiles from both companies. Automobiles are the wave of the future, don't you think? You might as well invest in something that could pay out twice over."

"I like the minds behind both companies," Agatha mused. "Innovators. They have their heads on straight, they work hard, they have bright futures. Would you invest more in Rolls-Royce or put some money towards Morris?"

Violet considered for a long moment and then said, "Some companies fail through sheer bad luck. They may both do well or perhaps one will fail and one will succeed. It might be better to diversify your investments."

"And my thoughts on the building in Manchester?"

"People have to live somewhere, Aunt Agatha. You know as well as I do that in a crowded city, your investment will pay out."

Agatha's mouth twisted. She didn't reflect approval or disapproval on Violet's comment.

"Do you like managing money?" Agatha made a note on the paper in front of her.

"Not particularly," Violet admitted. "I am rather spoiled, I suppose. I love to read my novels, spend time with my friends and family, pursue fashion, and perhaps I love nightclubs, jazz, and dancing more than I should."

"Perhaps you do," Agatha stated. "Yet when you wrote to me three months ago about investing in that shipment to America, you were clearly managing your money."

Violet nodded and said, "It paid out rather well. Victor and I took a good little profit from that."

"And your publishing company?"

"Gets our books in print," Violet smirked. "The ones that we write on the side of our magazine job."

"If you had something like Gerald has to manage, what would you do?"

"Something truly demanding like the estate?" Violet asked. "More than just Victor and I and our little asides?"

Agatha nodded.

"Please don't leave your money to me," Violet said suddenly. "I

don't wish to have something like Gerald has to manage. Aunt Aggie...
someone is trying to kill you for that pile of money."

"It's a gift."

"Is it? Surely not at the expense of your life," Violet said. "I love
you, Aunt Agatha. I don't want anything to happen to you."

"My dear girl, I intend on living for some time and I am not
offering you my fortune. I am merely curious about what you
would do."

"Intellectually only?"

"Intellectually only. A puzzle."

"To be honest, Aunt Agatha, I would find someone like Oscar
Harrison and hire him to manage the day to day. I'd only stick my nose
in often enough that he didn't get complacent. I would spend the rest
of my time traveling, spending too much money on clothes and jewels,
and probably continue to write stories with Victor. Though, at a less
frantic pace."

Agatha nodded again without showing approval or disapproval.

"Is this a game you're playing only with me?"

"No," Agatha said. "I am curious about the others' answers
as well."

"Will their answers change your decision about your fortune?"

Agatha leaned back again. This time her hands shook as she met
Violet's gaze. "It was to have been a gift. Henry and I wanted to create
it for our own children. When we weren't blessed and I lost my
Henry," Agatha's voice cracked and the old pain reflected in her gaze,
"it was what kept me going while I mourned him. I never stopped
mourning him, you know. And I never stopped growing this fortune
for those imaginary children. After a time, I looked around and realized that you were that child. You, Victor, John, all five of you. I didn't
think, not ever, that one of you would turn on me."

Violet's feelings had overcome her when Agatha's voice broke,
those feelings spilled down her face when Agatha said the rest.

"Please go on a trip," Violet said. "Leave in the nighttime. Go
somewhere wonderful and new. Meet a handsome man and have an
affair."

A watery laugh burst out of Agatha and she said, "You always were a troublesome thing. Full of too much vinegar. I understand you 'popped your top' at your uncle yesterday."

Violet's lips twitched and she admitted, "I did. I have been advised to flutter my lashes, flatter him effusively, and plead for forgiveness."

"It might work on that fool," Agatha said. Anger flashed in her gaze and she said, "He always did fall for every little female machination. Women don't even have to try that hard. He just assumes we're too stupid to pull the wool over his eyes."

Violet took a sip of her tea to avoid answering. She did not, however, disagree.

"Ah, the wise silence. You are a good girl, Violet. I am proud of you. I always have been."

Violet teared up at that. She picked up the letter opener again and rolled it across her fingers, focusing more on the etching in the handle than the look in her aunt's face. There was too much emotion in the room for a lighthearted afternoon of tea. Not that Violet had really expected such things since her aunt had announced someone was trying to kill her.

Someday soon, they'd sit down with tea and gossip. Violet would attempt, once again, to get her aunt to read some fun little novels, and Aunt Agatha would, once again, ignore Violet's banter about frivolous books. She couldn't really see Aunt Agatha ever reading one of the Tarzan novels or one of the books that were intended to terrify without focusing on edifying.

Perhaps they'd discuss fashion instead. They'd go shopping together and analyze the creations of the designers Violet loved. Aunt Agatha would buy a sturdy wool coat or perhaps a sensible sweater, and Violet would buy something silky and ridiculous. Violet's lips twitched at the idea and she looked up at her aunt, her gaze filled with so many emotions she didn't know how to qualify them in her heart.

What did her aunt see in Violet's face?

Whatever it was, she spurred, "Darling, I want you to know that the day your mother put you into my care was the day I started finding joy in my life again."

"Please don't," Violet whispered, clutching her hands so tightly her knuckles hurt.

"Don't tell you I love you?" Agatha's fierce face had softened probably as much as Violet's had.

"The issue is not the love, it's the feel of a goodbye."

"You and Victor and later John, Algie, and Meredith saved me, Violet. You children put joy back into my life. I've spent the last weeks looking back and thinking. I wasn't the best aunt. I wasn't fair. I am not fair now. My will is nothing but judgements and punishments. I believe it's time to correct that."

"What about a donation to one of those houses for the soldiers who prefer not to go out due to their scars? Those poor gentlemen deserve generosity more than any of us."

Aunt Agatha shook her head.

"A home for widows and children?"

At that Agatha's mouth twisted and she said, "I have less sympathy for widows than I should. I am one after all."

"The world would be a far different place if everyone was as fierce as you."

"Your mama was fierce like me. You are fierce like me. Now get out of my office and send me your brother or John Davies."

Violet stood, considered her aunt for a moment, and then rounded her desk to lean down and hug her fiercely.

"I love you, Aunt Agatha."

"And I you, my fierce girl. Tell whomever you send to give me a half an hour, will you?"

Violet was uncertain where she might find anyone, so she found Hargreaves instead. He was sitting at a solid looking table with Giles and a pot of tea in the butler's pantry. They both had their coats off and were working on polishing the silver while they lingered over their warm drinks. Violet immediately felt as though she'd invaded their space. They looked up at her knock on the door and then smiled at her. Hargreaves had set his coat to the side and he'd replaced it with an apron.

"I apologize for interrupting you, Hargreaves, Giles."

"Miss Violet, think nothing of it." He stood as he asked, "Whatever can I do for you, my dear?"

"I was hoping you'd know where either my brother or John is?"

"Your brother? I am afraid not. But I believe Mr. John is in the yellow room writing letters."

"Your brother is working in his rooms, miss," Giles added smoothly. "He seems to be harassed by his muse today."

That solved it. She'd hunt up John instead and maybe try to find out if he was trying to kill her aunt.

"Enjoy your tea, gentlemen. I apologize for interrupting." She left before they felt compelled to reply and made her way to the yellow room. It was one of the smaller parlors, but she recalled the desk in the corner. She'd used it herself many a time.

The yellow room had gold fleur-de-lis wallpaper arranged in rows with golden stripes separating each vertical row. The chairs and sofa were covered in golden fabric with large contrasting pillows. It seemed more as though someone had taken every yellow or gold piece of furniture and thrown it all in the same room with no thought beyond color. Yet, somehow, the room was bright and vivid rather than overwhelming.

John's red head was bent over the desk with such focus she was able to enter and take a seat nearby before he realized she was there.

"By Jove," he exclaimed when he saw her. "You are something of a sneaky thing. You should consider a future as a spy."

Violet laughed and then examined his face. "It's been some time, hasn't it?"

"Indeed," he agreed with an easy smile. He ran his hand over his jaw and crossed his legs.

"I didn't recognize you at first," she confessed. "I'd have thought I wouldn't be so thick with us all being here for Christmas as a family and yet...I am more of a dunce than I expected."

"You have changed quite a bit as well, and I believe the last time we spent time with Agatha together, I was nearly an adult, and you were 10 or 11. As I recall, you and your brother put itching powder in my bedsheets."

Violet barked a laugh and admitted, "We were the most horrible children."

John grinned and nodded and then said, "I believe you also put frogs in my bath."

She gasped and then remembered. "Oh goodness, we did. We'd challenged each other to catch more frogs than the other. Once I won, we decided we couldn't just let them go to waste."

John's deep chuckle rolled out across the room and he leaned back and said, 'Things are different this time."

"You've noted the tension," she said.

"Indeed. I've only seen Agatha here and there since I went to war. I didn't expect things to change so much."

"To be honest," Violet whispered, glancing over her shoulder as if looking for spies beyond herself. "Outside of this trip, you might have discovered Victor and I putting frogs in your bath again. I'm afraid we haven't matured much beyond our thirteenth year or so."

John laughed, but his question was serious when he asked, "What is going on, Violet?"

She flinched at the outright question, considered, and then said, "Aunt Agatha actually sent me for you. She wishes to have a private conversation. You have about a quarter of an hour before she expects you to present yourself in her office."

His mouth twisted up into another grin. That was the very term Agatha had used when they were being hooligans as children. "You won't shed some light on the mystery?"

Violet considered and then shook her head.

"Would you shed some light on your friend, Gwennie?"

Violet out and out grinned, rubbing her hands together before she asked, "Are you referring to my beautiful, sweet, well-connected friend Gwennie?"

The slew of adjectives were answers to questions he hadn't asked, and he smirked at her reply. "Indeed."

"Only if you answer your own questions first."

"Shoot."

The calculating side of Violet pressed to the forefront and she asked, "Do you have a good income?"

"Father was quite successful during the war," John said seriously. "I am well-set."

"More than capable of supporting a wife and educating children?"

"Very much so," he said confidently, and Violet considered. If he was truly interested in Gwennie, he wouldn't lie. It would ruin his chances with her, and it was so easily verifiable. It also very much lessened any need he might have to assist Aunt Agatha to the next life.

Their conversation had brought back old memories, too. Victor and Violet had tormented him. He had been so much older than them and yet he'd never retaliated or beat them within an inch of their lives as they'd deserved. Instead, he'd always laughed as though skin irritation from itching powder was somehow all in good fun. Could his life had changed so very much? His essential self? She didn't think so.

Her suspicion about him faded as she realized that he was a good man whose sight of the future was sidetracked by Gwennie. Those weren't the actions of some cold-blooded killer who was willing to take advantage of an old woman. Never.

"I'll be honest with you, John," Violet said. "You'll see more of us than you like should you end up falling for my friend. But you won't regret her even if you regret Victor and myself. She's sweet, and cleverer than she seems because she's so gentle and quiet. She's the type of woman who uses all that brainwork for the comfort of those she loves. She'll want you to dance with her and listen to music with her and spend long afternoons on a boat in the water, but if you can steal her heart away, she'll never stray. Not in her eyes, her mind, and never, ever in her heart."

John's head cocked as he said, "That is quite an endorsement."

"Lila and I might be closer friends, but both of us love Gwennie fiercely. Any man would be rich from having her love, and that my cousin, is the ring of the bell for Aunt Agatha."

John stood and said, "We'll talk again after I speak with Agatha. I don't care for the feel of things here, and I won't have her abused by your side of the family."

"Victor and I will join you in protecting Agatha."

"I never doubted it," John said. "I don't have the same confidence in that uncle of yours or that worm Algernon, but you and Victor always did love Agatha a little rabidly."

Violet laughed at his description and rose as he did. She followed him from the room and made her way to her brother. She couldn't leave all the work to him, and he'd be interrupted before long for his own conversation with Agatha.

CHAPTER SEVENTEEN

*T*he next morning everyone arrived at breakfast at the same time. Usually the spread was there and they came down as they pleased, serving up a plate from the sideboard and lingering over coffee and tea or the newspaper.

Perhaps it was the tension in the house. Dinner the previous evening had been near silent with only occasional quiet insults from Uncle Kingsley while the rest ate in silence and disappeared afterwards. Violet had worked through the night adding rather too much of their real life to the story they were writing, and she was exhausted when she sat down.

Uncle Kingsley didn't say a word while the rest of them made their plates. When Agatha appeared, his paper twitched, but he didn't fold it down. Algernon was even quieter, almost leaping out of his skin every time his father turned a page of the paper.

Aunt Agatha was pale as she seated herself at the table without a plate. "For those of you who are unaware, someone has been trying to kill me."

Gwennie dropped her teacup and flushed brilliantly, but no one said a word.

"This fiend has injured a lifelong friend of mine and driven me to an action I never anticipated making. I have sent for my lawyer. My will will change once he arrives."

"What's this now?" Uncle Kingsley demanded. "What are you up to, woman?"

Aunt Agatha left the room without deigning to answer. Violet dropped her napkin. Her gaze flit around the room and landed, finally, on Jack. He seemed entirely unsurprised. She stared at him until he turned her direction. His face was impassive, but Violet wondered just what the scheme was. She was almost certain, despite what Agatha had said, that something was afoot.

Beyond that, what bothered her most was the utter silence. No one protested. No one bemoaned. No one said a word.

Finally, Lila rose, jerked her head at Denny and they left the room.

"Does anyone know what has been happening?" John asked quietly. His jaw was tight and his eyes were blazing. Was it from the impending changes to the will or was it from the danger to their aunt?

Jack recapped each of the occasions that led to Aunt Agatha's conclusion. Laid out for all to review, it was as clear as day that someone had a target on Aunt Agatha.

"Seems to me she's seeing fairies where there ain't any," Uncle Kingsley said. "What's she gonna do? Throw all the money to the poor. I won't have it."

Victor leaned forward and said, "As much as you might like to lie to yourself about what is happening, that many near misses constitute a serious threat to Agatha."

Uncle Kingsley blustered and then said, "Don't be daft, boy."

"The poison, more than anything, shows exactly what we're dealing with," Violet replied.

"And you delivered that, didn't you?"

"There is no evidence," Jack snapped, "of any one person committing these crimes."

"I'm just saying the girl delivered the poison. Poison always was a woman's weapon."

Violet narrowed her gaze on her uncle. A woman's weapon? The only thing that required a woman specifically was birthing a baby. If he thought that a woman couldn't shoot a gun, he had another thing coming. If he thought a woman couldn't stab you in the back, he was very wrong. Perhaps it was assumed that poison was a woman's weapon because you didn't need to be strong to deliver it. Perhaps, if someone had tried to assault Agatha with a candlestick, it would require the strength of a man. But Violet would be damned if the suspects were narrowed only to herself and Meredith because they were female.

"The poison was delivered in sherry. Something that your aunt partakes of regularly and nearly exclusively," Jack stated clearly. Any doubts he had about Violet were not reflected in his defense of her.

"She could have done them all," Uncle Kingsley harrumphed.

"So could you," Jack said flatly. "Of all of you, Violet Carlyle is the one with the best motive for not killing Agatha. Unlike each of you, she has a legitimate offer of marriage from a man who makes Agatha seem like a pauper."

"What now?" Uncle Kingsley demanded. "I haven't heard of your engagement."

"I am not affianced," Violet stated and then lifted her tea to hide her smile at his reaction.

"Foolish girl," Uncle Kingsley countered. "Give the vote to women and they ruin their lives. What women need is a strong male hand at the reins."

"Leave my sister be," Victor said. "Her marriage or lack thereof is no concern of yours."

"And lucky she is," Kingsley said. "If she were mine, I'd set her straight, believe you me."

"It doesn't matter what you would do," Victor said, the lion in his gaze again. "Violet is not yours."

"Thank God for it! Probably a murderer. Delivering poison. Prancing about with good offers of marriage and frittering them away on stupidity."

"Kingsley, leave my sister be."

"Or what boy? So quick to defend your murderous sister."

"Unlike you," Victor roared, "Violet has not lost the fortune of her family. She still has the money she was given from our mother and as well as Grandfather. She has a good offer of marriage. She's beautiful and she's young and she's brilliant. She doesn't have to kill to have a bright future. When Agatha writes you out of the will, what will you do? Get a job? Please. There's nothing left for you."

"Victor!" Violet said softly. "Enough."

"Throwing accusations at each other gets us nowhere," Meredith said. "What are we going to do about Agatha changing her will?"

"Not a damned thing," John snapped. "She can do with her money as she likes and if she needs to change her will to save herself from some bedamned devil, so she will!"

"Hear, hear," Victor said.

Violet's gaze turned towards Algernon and Meredith, who were both silent in the face of such a reply. Meredith rose and left the breakfast room without another word. Algernon glanced at his father, still without breathing a word in his presence. The only way to describe Algernon's exit, a moment later, was a hasty retreat.

"You are a pack of simpering fools," Uncle Kingsley shouted. "All of you. Catering to the imaginations of a woman whose only claim to genius is sheer luck."

None of them bothered to argue with Kingsley about the clear and present evidence of a fortune to back Agatha's financial genius. Kingsley followed Meredith and Algernon from the breakfast room, slamming the door behind him.

John set down his coffee, staring after their uncle. "What the devil?"

How to reply? But John didn't need a response. He cleared his throat and then stated, "We will figure this out ourselves. I won't see my aunt lose her final years out of unadulterated greed. What do you know?"

To Violet's surprise, Jack explained what he'd learned so far. He didn't remove any of them from the suspect list, but John did. "You don't know these two. They've been wild, they've been rabid, they've been ridiculous."

Victor snorted and then said, "Hey now."

"And in all of that time, they have adored Agatha fiercely. She favors them, always has. Do you know why?"

Jack lifted his brows, waiting for an answer.

"Because they loved her as rabidly as she loved them. Meredith has always been a cold fish. Algernon was spoiled and entitled. I had my parents and didn't need Agatha. These two needed her as much as she needed them. I would bet the entirety of my not-unremarkable fortune that they'd sooner die than see her dead."

"It is my job to discover facts. The fact remains that there are many potential heirs and therefore many potential motives. I haven't been able to remove any of you from among my suspects, merely lower you. These crimes were too well thought out and didn't leave any evidence to pursue. Not yet. I'm trying to track the cyanide, but so far it's a fool's errand."

Gwennie was the one who said softly, "But surely there must be something. Surely you can see that Mr. Davies and my friends don't have a strong motive because they aren't exactly poor."

"It does," Jack admitted. "To be honest, Violet and John are barely on it. Victor has a little more motive without his own massive fortune and without the offer of one. My main suspects are Kingsley and Algernon. They'd have to be working hand in hand for the last two attempts, but it wouldn't be the first time a father and son worked together to commit crime."

Victor winced at that and then admitted, "Kingsley has always had Algernon cowed."

"Meredith's lot isn't enviable," Jack said, "but it's not so out of the ordinary. She's more fortunate than many a war widow."

Violet didn't argue with that, but she admitted that Meredith's fate was a nightmare.

"Didn't expect John to stand up for us like that," Victor said after Jack excused himself to check on his father and John excused himself to write some more letters. He was trying to keep up with his business concerns despite the visit.

"We had a good chat yesterday," Violet said. "He's intrigued by our Gwennie."

Victor shuddered a little and said, "Gwennie's delightful, but marriage is terrifying."

"John is quite a bit older than us, you child. We reminisced. Do you remember when we filled his bathtub with those frogs?"

Victor's laugh was answer enough.

"I want to see how easy it is to get from Gertrude's home to Aunt Agatha's," Violet told him.

"What's that?"

"Hargreaves said the train leaves at 10:00 a.m. I'm going."

Victor hesitated and then asked, "Shall we bring the allies?"

"We should leave Gwennie in John's tender care," Violet said. "You ask him to keep an eye on her given the machinations, and I'll get Lila to pretend to be ill so John gets a chance to know Gwennie unfettered of a chaperone."

"Are you matchmaking, you insufferable meddler?"

Violet smirked in reply and went to change her clothes. She selected boots to go with a wool dress and her coat and cloche before she found Lila and told her the plan.

"Being left behind was not the deal," Lila said. "But Denny wants to lay about and smoke anyway, and I've stolen the novels you hid in your trunk."

"It's for Gwennie," Violet said righteously with a pompous sniff. Lila slapped her arm and laughed and then admitted, "I have no desire to travel by train to an even smaller town just to snoop on your cousins, but you'll have to take me out for chocolates when we reach Paris."

"Consider it a date set in stone." Violet grinned and left before she could be trapped by Gwennie. Her friend might feel it was her duty to stand by Violet in her sleuthing instead of pursuing that fatal temptress, love.

They caught the train with Beatrice. "When we get there," Violet said. "I want you to gossip with anyone you can find who will talk to you. Tell them you got off on the wrong train and then ask if this is where Meredith Allyn lives. If they know her, chitchat with them. Start with nice comments. If they don't get you where you want, say vague mean things and see if anyone picks anything up."

Beatrice nodded, "Yes, miss. Of course."

They left her in the third-class compartment with money for lunch and enough to get home and then got themselves off the train. Violet purchased several things at the dress shop simply to have a reason to be in town and then they walked up to their cousin Gertrude's house.

"It's nicer than I imagined," Violet admitted. "The big windows, the lovely lawn. The hedges are so even."

"Were you imagining something with bars on the windows and a place in the cellar for Meredith?"

Violet's lips twitched as she confessed, "I suppose I was. She was so angry this morning about the will. For her, the reaction was on the level of Kingsley."

"She was much calmer than Kingsley, my luv," Victor said, casting Violet a surprised glance.

"Yes, but for *Meredith*. She's such a sour, cold thing. Kingsley is always blustering, so when he well and truly loses it, it isn't all that dramatic. But Meredith, she's not like that at all. So when she..."

"So when she has any reaction at all, you know she's upset."

"Do you think Aunt Agatha will leave it all to the widow's fund?" Victor asked as he knocked on the door.

"No," Violet said. "Yesterday she said her will was full of judgements and unfairness. She said she was setting it right. I suppose we're heirs after all; perhaps we'll split whatever she has evenly with the others?"

"Money just means that the pater and Eleanor will let up on me and focus on you. All that money and up for connections and what nots. They'll be dreaming of titles and castles for you, darling."

Violet winced and nodded. "Thinking that with money I've clawed my way off the shelf and burnished up my looks."

"Funny inn'it? How beautiful money makes a girl who's as long in the tooth as you."

Violet elbowed her twin as the door opened.

"Oh, hello," Victor said with a self-deprecating grin. "I know we're terribly unexpected and mannerless to show up like this, but my dear sister and I were shopping for Christmas when we realized our cousin, Gertrude, lived in this town. Didn't seem quite the thing to avoid saying our hellos."

The housekeeper eyed them distastefully and then asked, "Who should I say is calling?"

Victor didn't let the censure lessen his grin a bit as he said, "Victor and Violet Carlyle. We share a grandfather with Gertrude, don't you know? Poor thing to be related to mannerless duffs, like us."

"Hmm," the housekeeper said. A light drizzle started and she stepped back. "I'll inquire if she's home."

Violet's lips twitched again, but she otherwise kept her face expressionless. The housekeeper cleared her throat, cast them another censorious look, and then crossed to a parlor, entering, and precisely shutting the door behind her so the twins couldn't eavesdrop.

The entrance hall was respectable enough but the brightness of the outside didn't carry inside. A little dark, a little dank, and a little filled with prying eyes. Violet elbowed her brother and nodded towards the stairs where two sets of dark eyes peered down on them.

"Would you be the twins?" Victor asked brightly.

The eyes blinked once and twice and then a dirty little face appeared over the balustrade.

"Mebbe," the boy mumbled. A matching face popped up next to the first one and was, if possible, even dirtier than the first.

"Would you believe we're twins too?" Victor asked, giving the boys an engaging grin.

"Who'd want a girl for a twin?" the second twin asked. "Worse than not having a twin at all."

"So you'd think," Victor said while Violet scowled at them, "But Vi is a champion frog catcher, a teller of the spookiest tales, and she has a mean right hook." He'd changed how he normally spoke for the children, but they didn't seem to be reached.

"Dunnit," the first boy said.

"Does," Victor insisted, winking at the boys.

"Dunnit," the second boy said and then swore.

Violet gasped at the word.

While the first boy elbowed his twin and said, "See. Girls don't even let ya curse."

"Manners don't let you curse," Violet told the nasty imp with the same steady grin. "We've been visiting with your aunt, Meredith."

"Her," the second boy snarled. "Ugly stupid thing."

Victor placed a quelling hand on Violet and said, "Is she now? She used to catch frogs with me and my sister."

"You're a liar," the first twin said as the door to the parlor opened.

The housekeeper scowled at the twins and said, "Out of here, imps. Don't mind them. They're out of hand without Miss Meredith."

"Where is their nanny?" Violet asked brightly, pretending that she was unbothered by the little animals.

"The missus let her go when Miss Meredith moved in. Said with her sister around, she didn't need to fritter away money on nannies. Not my place, but Miss Meredith is no good with those boys. Course, no one is. They're Satan's imps disguised as children."

Violet paused despite the open door and said, "Meredith is providing nanny services?"

The housekeeper nodded and jerked her head towards the door, "The missus is waiting on you."

Victor met Violet's gaze and then led her into the parlor. Gertrude was older than them and they didn't know her well. She smiled when they came into the room and said, "What a delightful surprise."

Her smile did not reach her eyes.

Violet gave her a matching lie of a grin and said, "Well, we were just shopping for Meredith for Christmas and thought you might give us some ideas when we realized you were in town."

Gertrude scowled. "And how much longer does the old woman intend on keeping her?"

"Aunt Agatha?" Victor queried with a high-pitched tone.

"Threatening to remove Meredith from the will after all those visits and all that waiting on her. Thievery I call it."

Violet snapped her mouth shut before she said something she shouldn't while Victor let out a nervous, high-pitched giggle. Violet glanced at him, and he seemed as surprised at the noise he'd made as Violet.

"Father always said the rumors of her wealth were exaggerated. But he said it wasn't worth not pawning Meredith off on the old woman. Sort of an insurance policy, but we've never had much faith in the money."

Victor squeaked and Violet cleared her throat. Was this cousin of theirs playing a game with them? Violet had to battle off an overwhelming desire to reach out and poke Gertrude to see if this was some fairy dream.

"Did I...did I catch that right?" Victor asked, setting aside any attempt at manners in the face of Gertrude's venom. "Is Meredith your nanny?"

"Well...it's not like she's paying her way, is she?"

Victor blinked glanced at Violet and then turned back to Gertrude.

"Lives off our generosity, doesn't she? We feed her and even clothe her. The least she can do is help maintain the burden of this household."

"It was my impression," Violet said smoothly, "that nannies are paid."

Gertrude scowled at them and said, "One doesn't pay family for helping out."

Violet leaned back and looked at her brother, who looked sort of helplessly at her. They both turned to Gertrude and simply stared.

"Did you expect me to give you tea?"

"Indeed not." Victor rose and pulled Violet up after him. "Just wanted to say hello while we were in town. Hullo. We have a train to catch, don't you know. Happy Christmas and all that."

He didn't even wait for Violet to reply. Just left.

"One doesn't pay family for helping out," Victor quoted to Violet as they stepped down the stairs.

"She's an unpaid nanny, Vic," Violet whispered. "For those demons."

"I'm going to tell you the truth here," Victor said. "I might murder someone to escape that fate. But I don't think Meredith would."

Violet didn't answer that. She couldn't really imagine any of them as murdering their aunt. That was the problem with this whole situation.

Did Meredith have a motive? Only if they all did. Violet did. That money. That cursed money.

"I want to go home," Violet told Victor. "But we've never really had one, have we? Not with Eleanor at the homestead. Not with Agatha. It was never ours. The rooms...I suppose those are our home now."

Victor cupped her cheek and leaned his forehead down to hers. "I cannot promise you anything but this, sister of mine: you will never, ever be my unpaid nanny."

Violet looked up at him, and his lips twitched a little. His eyes were as haunted as she felt, but he joked for her. She hugged him tight and said, "Twin, sometimes I forget how lucky I am to have you."

"That goes both ways," Victor said.

"Why are you hugging your sister?"

Violet and Victor turned and faced the little devils. She shouldn't have done it. But after she was done, she didn't mind. She leaned down, putting her face into the first twin's and she whispered, "Do you know what happens to children who are mean to their aunts?"

He rolled his eyes at her as he scrunched up his nose.

"The shadow man comes for them." Violet's tone was all hoarse whisper. "He comes in the nighttime, when the candles go out, and the lights are off. He comes when the fire crackles, once, twice, and the wind blows from the east, and the child is lost forever to the darkness."

Both boys' eyes widened.

"The wind has been blowing from the east for the last few days hasn't it, Victor?"

He winced, giving the boys a trepidatious glance. "It has. It has."

"Do you want the shadow man to come for you?" Violet kept her voice low.

They shook their heads frantically. "Then you listen to your aunt. Women like Meredith know things. She's faced down the shadow man and won. Only a few have ever seen the shadow man and lived. Only. A. Few."

One of the boys shivered while the other clenched his fists. "Careful. I heard he got a kid a town over and he was moving this way."

One of the boys gasped, rubbing a grubby paw over his face and leaving a streak of dirt behind before he grabbed his brother and raced inside.

"You, precious one, are evil," Victor said lightly.

"Thank you," Violet said.

They found their way to an inn and bought a country luncheon and visited another shop before they caught the last train back to their aunt's home.

"I believe I overspent on Meredith," Victor confessed. "I bought her a shawl. Somehow I doubt they light a fire in her room."

"She's the specter in the attic," Violet said. "I bought her chocolates and perfume. I imagine she hasn't had a luxury since she was pawned off on that sister of hers."

"Poor kid," Victor said. Violet didn't disagree.

CHAPTER EIGHTEEN

*V*iolet watched the lawyer arrive with Victor standing behind her. Her bedroom overlooked the drive, and his car slowly putted up the drive before shuddering to a stop.

"I wonder if he'll make it home with that beast," Victor said. "Giles is good with a wrench for such a proper fellow. Do you think I should send him down and have him look the auto over?"

Violet shook her head and said, "Don't you men get a little touchy about other blokes making assertions on your manhood or vehicle?"

Victor grinned at her and tugged a hair before he admitted, "I hope this ends it all. I hope whatever trap Agatha has set up for us brings out the killer and we get back to some skating and a yule log."

"As do I," Violet admitted. "I stopped by Aunt Agatha's rooms this morning and last night, and she didn't answer. Her maid said that she wanted time to think and write."

Victor nodded and said, "I tried too. I wanted to talk to her about Meredith. About helping her out of there after this is all over."

Violet hadn't thought of that. She'd just wanted the touch of her mother—the closest thing she had to a mother—after seeing what a terrible family looked like. She turned back to her brother and said, "I never knew I should be so grateful for Gerald, Isolde, and Geoffrey. I miss Peter and Lionel more now."

Victor nodded and a flash of pain crossed his face. "Do you remember when Peter made us those kites? He spent the whole day with us outside? He was so much older, I thought he hung the moon."

Violet nodded and then said, "Do you remember how Lionel would send us novels after Eleanor said we couldn't have them? He used his own allowance for us."

"He was a good one. They both were."

"It's not fair that they're gone," she said. "That stupid war took so much from us."

"It's not fair that we have each other *and* had them while Meredith only has that shrew."

Violet winced for Meredith again, feeling guilty that they hadn't been better to her. "Should we go down to breakfast?"

"I suppose we have to despite Uncle Kingsley."

"Do you really think he's trying to kill Aunt Agatha?"

Victor hesitated and then said, "He's got nothing left, Vi. He probably feels trapped. Many men have fallen on the sword, so to speak, once they got where he is. I'm sure he's thought of it. Perhaps he decided to throw her on the sword instead."

Violet flinched at that thought and then said, "Life is cruel."

"Sometimes," Victor agreed.

Victor loaded up a plate of kedgeree, beans, tomato, fried potatoes, and toast. Violet made a plate of fruit, tomatoes, and toast. She considered the tea before she decided upon coffee. When she sat down across from Meredith, Violet winced and then asked, "How did you sleep, cuz?"

The light-hearted banter was as forced as laughter during an execution. Victor winced for Violet and nodded at Jack who folded his paper and watched Violet.

"I didn't sleep," Meredith said, and she looked it. She had bags under her eyes and dark circles as well. She moved almost as if she hurt. "Aunt Agatha is changing her will after years of leading us to believe we might inherit a little something. I'm not happy someone is trying to hurt her, but they've stolen from all of us now."

Violet forced an image of Gertrude to the forefront of her mind before she said, "We don't know how she's going to change it, dear."

Meredith's mouth twisted as she said, "I just thought...I thought it would be different."

Her plate was full and untouched. Only her teacup had been emptied.

"Would you like to go skating tomorrow? Hargreaves said the pond is frozen enough."

Meredith didn't even reply. She just rose and said, "Excuse me."

The moment she was gone, Jack turned to Violet and asked, "What was that?"

"We saw where she lives yesterday," Victor said. "Her sister is... there aren't words. I write stories and make money at it, and there aren't words for it."

"You two need to stay out of this investigation," Jack told them. "What did you go to Shelby for? To see Meredith's motive or lack thereof for yourself? If she's the killer, Victor, you've just put a target on your own back *and* your sister's."

Victor shoved some food in his mouth before he said, "I'll miss Cook when we go home. But, like you, Vi—I ache for my own bed and the comfort of the familiar. I believe, however, I promised you Paris and then Italy. Possibly America."

Jack precisely folded his paper, scowling at them for not even acknowledging his reprimand and then asked, "America?"

"Not America." Violet felt the caress of Jack's gaze on her, and suddenly she didn't want to be gone quite so long. She simply...found something more intriguing in London. "But a few weeks in Italy with the sun and the sea does seem about right."

"We'll go to America next year," Victor said oblivious to the tension between Jack and Violet. "Or perhaps Switzerland. I'd like to ski the Alps."

Violet took another sip of her coffee and then popped a grape from the orangery into her mouth. It was divine. She made no promises about America or the Alps.

"The lawyer has arrived?" she asked Jack even though she knew the answer.

He nodded and said, "He's working in the yellow room, gathering his thoughts and waiting until she's ready, and then meeting with Agatha."

Just as Jack finished his statement an unholy shriek filled the air.

"Oh, God no," Victor said.

Violet dropped her coffee. It clattered against the side of the table and crashed onto the floor, shattering and spraying herself and Victor with a rain of dark beverage.

Violet said nothing, but her head was shaking back and forth without stopping. She couldn't move, she couldn't think. She didn't need to think to know what the shriek heralded. Victor grabbed her hand and hauled her out of the breakfast room behind Jack who had already disappeared.

Aunt Agatha's office door was open and Mrs. Daniels had collapsed in the doorway, blocking the entrance. Jack seemed to have leapt over the housekeeper while Hargreaves was patting Mrs. Daniels's face.

Violet didn't want to look. The expression of Hargreaves's face told her all she needed to know. In the game of chess against a would-be-killer, they had lost.

"No!" Violet said. "No! I know there was a plan. I know that...damn it. The plan was supposed to have stopped this!"

Victor took her by the shoulders and turned her to him. She looked up at him and asked, "Is it too late? Is she gone?"

He didn't speak, his jaw was bound too tightly in fury, but his nod gave her the answer she needed, killing the last of her hope.

"But there was a plan. Why would Agatha not have a plan? She thought out everything."

"I don't know," Victor whispered. "I don't know what happened."

Their friends followed the sound of shouts and Violet looked up, meeting Lila's gaze. She examined them as John Davies raced into the hall and then Meredith, Algernon, and finally Uncle Kingsley.

"What's all this then?" Uncle Kingsley demanded.

"She's gone," Victor said and then swore.

Uncle Kingsley took a step back as though some unseen force had shoved him and he said, "But. Well. That can't be right."

Hargreaves got Mrs. Daniels to her feet. She was weeping almost frantically and Lila crossed to her, wrapping her arms around the woman who had worked for Agatha through all of Violet's life.

"Come with me," Lila whispered. "Come on now."

"It can't be right, I say," Uncle Kingsley shouted.

"I assure you, it is," Jack said, shutting the door to Agatha's office behind him. "Hargreaves...call the police. Tell them Chief Inspector Jack Wakefield is here and have them contact Scotland Yard. I'll need whomever they have and the doctor as well."

Hargreaves nodded and rushed into the library where the telephone was kept.

"The police! Chief Inspector! You here in sheep's clothing, you— you—wolf!" Uncle Kingsley's voice echoed through the huge house.

Violet had enough. She turned on her uncle and said, "He's here because Aunt Agatha asked him to be."

"Well, we've lost her, haven't we?" Meredith said. "He wasn't very successful."

"We lost her," Violet shouted, "because she refused to leave and be safe. Because she refused to take the *coward's way*. Foolishness! We lost her because some greedy mongrel decided their desire for a new dress or fine house was worth murdering a woman who had loved us all of our lives. Unworthy fools that we are."

"Who are you calling a greedy mongrel?" Uncle Kingsley demanded, ruddy fury rising high in his face. He'd have loomed over Violet if Victor didn't have her tucked under his arm.

"You!" she shouted. "You! You wanted her money. You were demanding it yesterday. As if she owed you for your own idiocy."

Uncle Kingsley's infuriated splutter had Meredith stepping back rapidly while Algernon winced.

"You've done it now, cuz," Algie said, almost apologetically.

"Enough!" Jack said. "Mr. Allyn, remove yourself from this hall immediately."

"Who do you think you are?"

"The man who will be finding your aunt's murderer and seeing them to justice."

Uncle Kingsley blustered for a moment and then he spun and strode from the hall.

Jack turned to survey the gazes that were fixed on him and then he said, "Mr. Coates, I will need to speak with you, but..."

Violet started and her manners came to the forefront. There in the shadows was a little man with round glasses and a brown suit. Aunt Agatha's lawyer had arrived and seen the family battle. Violet wiped away a tear and tried to speak. Her first attempt came out as a croak and then she said, "Take the yellow room again," finding her control. "I'm...oh..." She didn't even realize she was speaking through her tears until Jack handed her a handkerchief.

"Is she really gone?" John Davies asked. "It doesn't seem possible."

"Yes," Jack snapped. "Yes. Damn it. Yes, she is. We had someone watching the hall to see if anyone came in, but whoever it was went through the window. She's almost cool. The damned killer must have found her almost as soon as she went into the office."

"When we were all without an alibi in our bedrooms," John snarled. "She came down before breakfast, didn't she? Give us all our chance to kill her."

Hargreaves returned and said, "Sir, I didn't leave my post once. Not once."

"You didn't have to," Jack said. "We didn't think of the window. We should have. We assumed the killer wouldn't know it was a trap."

"But I did remember the window, sir. I checked the locks on it just last night. Those are sturdy locks. We replaced them only a year ago when a few of the larger houses were broken into."

"Then the killer had planned this well enough to wait for you to check them, unlock it, and slide in while we were watching the wrong damn door."

Violet stared at Hargreaves. How many times had she and Victor snuck down to the kitchens for biscuits and been caught by Hargreaves as he was fixing the locks. She was sure the rest of the cousins would know the same. Of course they would.

"That was your trick, wasn't it? As children, you two would wait

until Hargreaves checked the locks and then sneak out for your...
escapades." Meredith insinuated. Her gaze was fixed on Violet as
though she had been the one who would have killed Aunt Agatha.

"As children," Victor said, the muscle in his jaw flexing.

"You were terrible children," Meredith said. "You are, no doubt,
terrible adults."

"Enough," Jack told Meredith. "You will go to the parlor or your
bedroom until I need to speak with you. I will follow the evidence and
we will find the killer with proof and deduction. Not with random
accusations based off of behavior from a decade ago."

Violet slowly turned to him and asked one more time, "She's really
gone?"

"She is," Jack said gently.

He didn't need to tell her to go to her room. She fled there, blindly,
with tears rolling down her cheeks.

CHAPTER NINETEEN

*P*erhaps if Uncle Kingsley had less motive, he'd have tried to pull out the power of classes. Jack Wakefield wouldn't have succumbed as easily as any other detective. He was of their class. He might not have an earl for a father, but his father was connected to the landed families with a fortune behind him and membership in the right clubs—antiquated though they were.

That might be unfair to Scotland Yard detectives, however—maybe none of them would give way in the face of threats. Not in this day, and this age. But in another house, at another time, it would have gone that way. Especially with another investigator. It helped rather a lot that Jack Wakefield was a well-connected man who'd learn to investigate during the war and then chosen to join Scotland Yard later because of his skills rather than a need for money. Men like Uncle Kingsley, Algernon, and even Victor would have fallen back on their money rather than work.

Victor followed Violet to her bedroom and then entered after her.

"I'm not leaving you alone, luv," he said when she told him to leave.

"I just need..."

"No," he said firmly. "No. One of our cousins or perhaps Uncle

Kingsley murdered Aunt Agatha. You are with me, Lila, or Denny until the killer is caught. Not even Gwennie. She's too...passive."

"Vic..."

"Violet, we've lost Mama, Peter, Lionel, Baby Iris, and now Aunt Agatha. I can survive with all of that, but I'll be damned if I lose my twin to some animal who wants a larger inheritance."

"Then you will do the same? You'll stay with someone?"

"I am a man," he said.

"And if the killer has a gun? Or if it's Algernon who has five stone on you?"

Victor smirked and then said, "You know that's all baby blubber."

Violet laughed through her tears and then curled up on her bed. She wanted her aunt. She wanted to curl up in Aunt Agatha's lap, just as Violet had done when they'd heard word that Peter had gone down only three weeks into his service as a pilot during the war. She wanted to feel Aunt Agatha's fingers running through her hair as she talked about the next life and the peace of heaven. Of what a good brother he'd been. Only this time she'd have to talk about those things by herself.

Violet imagined her aunt's voice. *All is well, darling. I've missed Henry so. Now I am with him. With my mama and yours. In a better place. At peace.*

What a loving aunt Agatha had been...how generous with the little motherless twins despite how naughty they'd been. A sob escaped Violet, and her brother climbed onto the bed next to her. He placed a hand on her shoulder while she cried. He wasn't Aunt Agatha. He didn't know she needed more than a hand. She needed whispered assurance and the promise of better things to come.

The journey from tears to sleep happened so seamlessly she wasn't aware of it until someone knocked on the bedroom door. She started and Victor pushed himself from the bed, crossing to open it. On the other side, a white-faced, red-eyed Beatrice whispered. Victor nodded and Violet closed her eyes again. She didn't care why they were at the door or what they wanted.

A few minutes later, Victor said, "Mr. Coates and Jack have decided that they will read the will now. Both the old one and the one Aunt Agatha never got to enact. They want our presence."

Violet slowly sat up. She winced. She'd forgotten how it hurt to lose someone. How the pain traveled from your heart to your extremities, and your very muscles seemed to protest the loss.

"They need you too, luv. Mr. Coates said that all the main recipients need to present."

"So all of us, then?"

Victor shrugged and admitted, "I have no idea. Just that Beatrice was sent for both of us."

Violet crossed to the bath and washed her face. She didn't care so much about her looks, but the splash of water on her face helped her to wake up. She ran a brush through her hair more out of habit than anything else. As she glanced at herself in the mirror, the powder blue dress she was wearing seemed so very inappropriate. She exited the bath, saw Victor, and then crossed to grab a grey dress with long sleeves.

It seemed the best choice given what had happened. Her red number or that champagne gown mocked the loss she'd suffered. Violet changed in the bathroom, slipped on her shoes, and let Victor lead her downstairs. She knew her brain was on hiatus. She felt rather like she'd stepped into a cloud and couldn't get out of it.

"I...I need coffee," she told Victor. "I can't think."

He nodded and took her to the kitchen where she gulped some coffee and then met the others in the library. There were two chairs near the fire for Jack and Mr. Coates. Several others were circled in front of them. Jack held a notebook and a uniformed constable was in the room with another notebook.

Victor seated Violet in a chair to the side and glanced around. It seemed that everyone else had beat them to the room. Meredith was stone faced and calm. John Davies was seated with his gaze fixed on the floor, jaw clenching. Hargreaves and Mrs. Daniels stood at the back of the room, while Algernon and his father were seated at the forefront of the room directly in front of the lawyer.

There was another chair, for Victor, across the room, but he stood next to Violet with his hand on her shoulder. A moment later, Hargreaves moved the chair next to Violet and Victor nodded his thanks.

"Well..." Mr. Coates said. His face was white and he cleared his throat. "My purpose here today was to change Mrs. Davies's will. However, her death happened before changes could be made making her most recent will the one in effect. This will is dated the first of July, 1922."

No one said a word, but several bodies shifted in their seats. Violet didn't look to see who was moving about. If only Aunt Agatha had just gone to the Amalfi coast. Christmas in Italy would have been lovely. The sun would have shone down on her aunt's white hair, and she might have become terrifically brown.

"I will now read the will which was written by Agatha Margaret Davies and witnessed by myself, Hargreaves, and my clerk, John Hammond."

"My darlings," it started and Violet could almost hear her aunt's voice instead of Mr. Coates.

"My late husband, Henry, and I once set about in a game. It was, you see, to create a fortune to hand over to our children. When we weren't blessed with our own young ones before I lost dear Henry, I determined to stay the course of our game. Since then, I worked on increasing my fortune as a gift for one of you. I was never not looking for the best recipient. Perhaps Henry's nephew? Perhaps Algernon? Perhaps young Victor who wasn't anyone's main heir? Perhaps I would choose instead one of my nieces. After all, of all women, I knew that a woman was as capable as a man in learning to manage and grow a gift such as the one I was creating.

"In order to determine the best recipient, I made a list of things that I would like to see my children—you—do. I wanted to see you educated. Not just at the university but in life. I have given each of you the chance for an education. Only Victor and Violet took advantage of that offer and graduated. Algernon, your performance at school was dismal. John, of course I excuse you in the service of our country."

Violet sniffled into a handkerchief.

"I have loved each of you, but as I grew this fortune, I wanted to see that I could turn it over to good stewards. Those who would protect and grow it for the next generation. To transform my gift to a legacy."

Violet lifted a shaking hand to her lips, remembering those times when Aunt Agatha had seen to that very education she was speaking of beyond the grave. Or beyond wherever they'd placed Agatha's body. Violet felt a tear slip down her face and ignored it. This moment seemed to be the last time she'd ever hear her aunt's voice even if it came through Mr. Coates.

"Each of you knows now, looking back, how you fared in that education. I, Agatha Davies, being of sound mind and memory, do hereby declare this to be my last will and testament, thereby revoking and making void any and all other last will and testaments made by me."

"To my brothers, Kingsley and Cecil, I leave nothing but my love, such as it is."

Uncle Kingsley swore and Mr. Coates stated, "That is quite enough."

To Violet's shock, her uncle didn't snap back.

"To my beloved nephew, John Davies, I leave thirty thousand pounds, the home purchased by his Uncle Henry, as well as the personal library and effects of my late-husband, John Henry Davies."

Uncle Kingsley shifted enough that Violet could see his fingers twitch. She was sure he was calculating in head what Algernon might inherit. Did Kingsley know the value of Agatha's estate? Violet didn't. Victor didn't. She wanted to shout at Kingsley that he was taking Agatha's voice from her head, but she said nothing.

"To my beloved nephew, Algernon. You are both a joy and a disappointment."

Algernon said nothing, but he did squeak.

"You have not graduated from university, you have not worked, you did not take the opportunity I presented for either a job or to learn how to manage my money; however," Mr. Coates paused and Algernon leaned forward.

Violet clutched her fingers together to hide their shaking.

"You have always been kind. I have seen endless acts of generosity even when you were hard-up yourself. You are, my boy, deplorable with money. Therefore, I leave you a trust of twenty-thousand pounds and access to the interest. Care of that trust will be seen to by Coates, Coates, and Landon."

Uncle Kingsley cursed again. Aunt Agatha left to each of Algernon's siblings, three thousand pounds each when they turned twenty-five and an education if they desired to pursue it.

"To my niece-in-law, Helen Allyn, I leave a house purchased for you in Surrey."

Uncle Kingsley's eyes closed and he breathed deeply when his wife received. Violet's face turned towards him, and she could swear she saw relief in his face.

"To my niece Gertrude, who has transformed her sister into a servant, I leave nothing."

"To my niece, Meredith, I leave the interest of 10,000 pounds and access to the full funds on her thirty-fifth birthday."

Meredith gasped but said nothing. Was it the lesser amount of money that bothered her?

"To my beloved nephew, Victor, you did not pursue an education either at the university or with me with any measure of vigor. However, you learned enough to get by. You used your greater inheritance to provide your twin, Violet, with freedom that many other young men would not have. You always protected her and loved her with the same feeling you extended to myself."

Victor's arm was wrapped around Violet's shoulders, and she could feel his tension and then a slight relaxing as Aunt Agatha's approval was announced.

"I leave you, Victor Carlyle, one-half of the remainder of my fortune, my house in London, and my endless love."

Victor squeezed Violet's shoulder but said nothing. How much was what? Violet didn't think either of them really knew. Uncle Kingsley wasn't all that happy to hear what Victor had received. Because he excelled where Algernon failed?

"And my beloved, Violet Carlyle. I suppose favoritism is both unfair and inevitable. But of my nieces and nephews, it was only you who read the reports and learned from me. To you, I leave the remainder of my funds, possessions, and homes. This inheritance includes the apartment in Paris, the house in the Lake Country, and the villas in Italy and France. I leave my jewelry and art collections as well as all remaining sundries and business interests. I enfold into your care my beloved

Theodore Hargreaves and Juliette Daniels. I know you will see to them well, though to each of them, I leave 500 pounds. To my reliable cook, I leave 200 pounds. To each of the remaining servants on my staff, I leave 20 pounds."

Mr. Coates cleared his throat and then said, "To each of you there is also a letter. Smaller items have been left to a few friends, but this is the will in bulk."

Violet's hands were shaking as Uncle Kingsley turned on her.

"Did you know?"

"Know what?" Victor asked, stepping in front of her.

"Know that Agatha was playing some training game as though a few reports on coffee beans or manufacturing in Leeds will pass on the golden touch. Agatha was...was...just blessed."

Violet didn't bother to answer.

"Twenty thousand pounds for Algernon and a house for your wife is nothing to sneeze at," Victor told Kingsley.

"And what did she leave me? Not a damned thing!"

"You probably should have treated her better," Algie said, "if you wanted her money."

"What's that, boy?" Kingsley turned on his son, fists clenched, but Algernon slowly stood.

"You told me to ignore Agatha's report. You told me that she was a fool woman. You told me that a degree from the university was worthless beyond connections. You were the one who introduced me to Theodophilus and gambling."

Victor squeezed Violet's hand. She slowly, quietly asked, "What did the new will say? The one that would have changed things?"

"That's an interesting thing," Mr. Coates said. "She split the money evenly between the five of you, agreed to pay off Mr. Kingsley Allyn's debts. It still favored you some, as she still left you the jewelry and art as well as control of her company."

"Excuse me?" Meredith asked.

"There weren't any delays on the funds either. After death duties, you'd all have been able to do as you wished with the funds."

Uncle Kingsley laughed at that. A hysterical laugh that prodded

Violet out of her chair, up the stairs, and into her bedroom. She slammed her bedroom door, locked it, and then turned to face her bed.

Her aunt had been murdered, Violet had inherited a rather vast amount of money. She'd never have to write another story again and all of the sudden, she wanted nothing more than to destroy a villain on the pages of her manuscript and slide back into the time when her aunt yet lived.

CHAPTER TWENTY

*L*ila and Gwennie knocked on the bedroom door while Violet lay curled onto her side. She answered the door and her friends were accompanied by Beatrice with a tray of sandwiches and another housemaid who held a tray with coffee, biscuits, and fruit.

"You have to eat," Lila said. She glanced around the room and said to Beatrice, "Would you mind terribly straightening her room? Violet can't stand it when things aren't just so."

Beatrice nodded and started cleaning while Lila poured Violet a cup of coffee, added a stiff shot of whiskey from a flask tucked under her arm, and then placed a plate of sandwiches in her lap.

"You have to eat," Lila told Violet firmly.

Violet blinked her friend's way and shrugged.

"If you don't eat, I'll call for Victor."

Violet stared and then slowly lifted the sandwich and took a bite. She tasted nothing, but she choked it down. About halfway through the sandwich, she stopped trying and Lila didn't object.

"What happened?" Lila asked.

"I think I might be swimming in money," Violet admitted. "I am certainly swimming in jewelry and art. I inherited an apartment and house I didn't even realize Aunt Agatha owned and two villas. Victor inherited the London house. John got rather a lot of money and this old heap."

"I'd congratulate you," Gwennie said. "But I know at least you, John, and Victor would rather have Agatha."

"I inherited a percentage, so...I don't really know how much money I have. Maybe I'm wrong. Maybe I don't have anything."

"Well, it hardly matters, does it?" Lila asked pushing Violet's doctored coffee at her again. "Yesterday, you were happy with what you had. Today you have more."

"Oh, I didn't think of it like that," Gwennie said.

"They'd set this whole thing up," Violet said. "Jack and Aunt Agatha. The announcement of the will changing, the way Aunt Agatha disappeared into her office. Hargreaves was watching the door to see who tried anything, but no one did."

"Then...."

"Someone unlocked the window to the office last night and slipped in this morning and killed her. I don't even know how she died..."

Lila shifted and said, very softly, "She was stabbed in the back with her letter opener. The doctor said she didn't suffer."

Violet didn't realize she'd started crying again until Lila brushed back her hair and wiped her face with her handkerchief before she said, "It'll be all right, luv." Her voice was low and soothing. "It's horrible now, and it's not fair. But you are lucky. You had someone who loved you so much."

Violet nodded against Lila's shoulder as she said, "I didn't realize how much I loved her. Not until she was gone. I can't...I don't...I don't want the money. She was my mother in all the ways that mattered."

There was another knock on the door and Beatrice opened it. Hargreaves stood on the other side. His face was pale and he had the look of someone who'd seen something terrible. Given he'd discovered the body of his mistress, he had. "The police need fingerprints, Miss Violet. Mr. Jack Wakefield apologized to interrupt your grieving, but he needs them sooner rather than later."

Violet turned and said, "Lila said Aunt Agatha was stabbed with her letter opener."

"I'm afraid that is correct, miss," Hargreaves said. Mr. Jack Wakefield is working in the library with the local constables."

"My fingerprints are on it," Violet told Hargreaves. She sounded exhausted. She felt wrapped in wool and pain. "I opened Agatha's letters yesterday while we talked in her office. I have a hard time with messes and her mail was scattered across her desk."

"Your fingerprints are on the murder weapon?" Hargreaves's jaw tightened and then he said, "Miss Violet, Mrs. Davies asked Mr. Jack to help her because he is very good at what he does. There is no need to fear."

"I hope that's true," Lila said fiercely. "If it isn't, we'll just...bribe officials with your fortune."

"I don't think she'll receive the money, if they think she killed Mrs. Davies," Gwennie said softly.

"Victor will though," Lila said. "No need to worry."

Violet felt a flash of fear. "It can't be good for me that my fingerprints are on the weapon."

"We'll find the real killer," Lila swore.

Violet nodded, wrapping a shawl around her shoulders. She hadn't been so cold perhaps at any time. Her fingers hurt with the pain of the cold despite the fires burning throughout the house. She followed Hargreaves down the stairs and into the office where Jack was working with the constable.

"Mr. Wakefield," she said softly. "I used the letter opener yesterday when I was speaking to Aunt Agatha."

His jaw tightened and he nodded. He was the one who took her fingerprints. He did it with careful, large hands that made her shiver though she wasn't quite sure why. Despite the fact that he was compiling evidence against her, she still felt safe.

"The will would have changed out of my favor too. That can't be good."

His jaw flexed over and over and then he said, "You didn't know that. There is far more motive for your uncle to have injured your aunt. He is still at the end of things. Perhaps he realized that he wasn't in either will. Perhaps he acted out in rage."

The constable, Officer Jones, was baby faced with blond hair and dark eyes. He nodded at what Jack said. Was the young constable so certain then? Did she know him? She couldn't recall his face.

"Thank you for telling me," Jack said. "Make a note of it, Jones."

Did Jack believe she'd killed Aunt Agatha? Was that note of Jones to show she was helpful? To weaken or strengthen the case against her should it come before the court? She wanted to believe he knew her better than any idea that she might be a killer.

But, the simple fact was he didn't know her well at all. He didn't know her favorite music or food. He didn't know if she liked to ride horses or whether she was a good dancer. All he knew was that she'd had some expectation of inheritance and may have killed her aunt.

"Lila said Aunt Agatha didn't suffer."

"It is hard to say," Jack said. "But I believe she died quickly. She didn't have time to cry out or seek help. That is a good sign that she didn't suffer."

Violet found she was crying again and that Jack kept a clean hand-kerchief in his pocket. He pressed it into her hands and asked, "Did you know you were her heir?"

"Haven't we discussed this before? I didn't know. I knew she was rich," Violet admitted, woodenly. "But I wouldn't have thought she had quite that much money. I don't even...I mean...how much did I inherit?"

Jack's head turned towards her and he said, "She did leave it to you in percentages, didn't she? One-half of what was left. I don't really know. Jones, fetch Mr. Coates."

Victor came into the room with Mr. Coates and said, "I'm not sure it's quite the thing to be interviewing my sister alone."

Violet scowled at her brother and said, "Enough of that."

"Vi, we're talking actual murder here. A possible hanging."

"The murder investigation is not over," Jack said. "Don't leap to conclusions that aren't warranted. What we need to know, Mr. Coates, is exactly what these two inherited."

Mr. Coates adjusted his glasses and stepped into the library. "As of right now, my clients are the heirs. I work for them, not you, Mr. Wakefield."

"Tell him," Violet said. "Just tell him."

"Violet," Victor hissed.

"Victor," Violet snapped. "Aunt Agatha is dead. We aren't going to make it harder to find her killer."

"Who might have set you up! We all got something. Maybe something worth killing for. Maybe it's better to have the lesser amount of money and pin the crime on some other cove!"

"Mr. Coates," Violet said. "Please answer whatever questions Mr. Wakefield and the police might have regarding Aunt Agatha's estate." Violet nodded at the constable and Jack as she said, "If you no longer need me..."

"Wait!" Victor called. "I don't want you wandering the house until the killer is caught."

"Don't be silly, Victor. Right now, I'm the killer's favorite person. My fingerprints are on the weapon, I handed Aunt Agatha a cupful of poison, I inherited..." She turned to Mr. Coates and asked, "Did I inherit the most?"

"Ah...well..." Mr. Coates glanced at Victor and then said, "By a rather wide margin. The split of her remaining money, itself, was very even between you and your twin. But your aunt left you her shares and interests in her business dealings. Those are worth...quite a bit."

"See," Violet said. "The only person left with a motive to hurt me is you. You're my heir, my lad."

He almost snarled at her, but she left him in the library and slowly walked up the stairs to her room. What had he said? Something was bothering her. She passed Uncle Kingsley's room at the front of the stairs and noted that it was being thoroughly searched by two of the local police.

Violet slowly passed the room, taking full advantage of the chance to look inside. She didn't even try to hide what she was doing, but they didn't note her interest. What *had* Victor said that had caught at her mind? That it was better to inherit less but have someone else seem like the killer.

Here they were searching Uncle Kingsley's rooms. He seemed like a likely killer. Almost as much as Violet. Uncle Kingsley had lost so much, he was in dire straits. Far more so than the rest of them. Could it be him?

She went into her room and took up the list of suspects she'd made that first night. She took the list over to her desk and pulled out a new sheet of paper.

Slowly she wrote the names again and considered them in the new light.

JOHN DAVIES— Seems well off. Maybe not as rich as Agatha, but rich enough. He also seems as though he were quite fond of Agatha. He inherited well, but it won't change his life in any way. Killer? Not in my opinion.

ALGERNON ALLYN — He is in the soup. He doesn't have a lot of money and his dad lost everything. But, Aunt Agatha's will gave him money despite his foolishness because he was kind. Could she have been so wrong?

Violet didn't want to believe that Agatha had been wrong about Algie. When you came right down to it, he was well-connected and handsome enough he could probably marry some nouveau riche daughter or use his connections to get a job. Algie...his plan to marry Violet off...it wasn't the plan of someone who was bright. It was the plan of someone who hadn't given up hope. Violet just didn't think Algernon had done it.

What about Kingsley?

KINGSLEY ALLYN — Before the will and before he'd arrived, Violet had thought he had his own money. She hadn't been aware he'd lost everything. When had that occurred? Before or after the first murder attempt. It had been weeks and weeks ago, hadn't it? The way he'd acted since he arrived had been downright belligerent. He had been awful to everyone, especially Agatha. Did he really believe that he could bully her into keeping her will the same? But...he hadn't even been in the will. Not either one. Not really. Though the second will did pay off his debts.

Violet tapped her finger against her notes. It was in the opposite of his best interests to kill her before the will had changed. Was he really so sure he'd inherit something from his aunt? After all their many battles? After he'd seen his own brother disinherited?

Violet's mouth twisted. She knew that Uncle Kingsley had hoped his aunt would rescue him and his family. Only Aunt Agatha wasn't that type of woman. She was almost cold when it came to business. He knew that. Violet knew that. If Aunt Agatha couldn't be persuaded to save him, would he have killed her in a rage?

Violet thought about how Aunt Agatha had died. Someone had planned to do it from the time she'd said the lawyer was coming to update the will. Someone wanted to avoid Aunt Agatha from changing the will. Whoever had killed Agatha both expected something in the will and felt it was worth killing over. Were they concerned they'd be removed from the will? She'd never said what she was going to do, so why would anyone jump to that conclusion? Maybe, they were really worried that she'd leave the money to a charity instead of her nieces and nephews.

Violet slowly rose and walked down to the kitchens. She found Cook working quickly and Hargreaves in his shirtsleeves.

"I'm sorry," Violet said, "to intrude on your space. I...Hargreaves, did you ever think of anyone who might have known or been here when Aunt Agatha made her will the last time?"

Hargreaves shook his head and Cook said, "Miss Meredith was here. I remember it clearly. She'd been blue and I perked her up with some jellies while Mr. Coates was with Mrs. Davies."

"Meredith?" Violet hadn't even put Meredith on the list when she'd been up in her room.

"Your aunt had been worried about Miss Meredith. Mrs. Davies had me make some heartening foods to get the blood up. Even had the doctor out. You remember Hargreaves, the doctor said Miss Meredith was exhausted."

He blinked quickly and said, "Oh yes. I remember now. I apologize Miss Violet, I—"

"I'm sure it's of no import," Violet said. "Mr. Wakefield and the constables are focused on myself and Uncle Kingsley."

"You?" The cook laughed, but she didn't sound amused. It was the bark of fury before she said, "You'd sooner kill your brother than Mrs. Davies."

"I didn't, of course. I would never." Violet was seated at the table with a cup of tea and a plate of biscuits while Cook fussed over her.

She muttered as she worked, "What's the world coming to? I ask you! I ask you, Hargreaves? People killing a good woman like Mrs. Davies for what? Filthy lucre. Filthy lucre. It's a cold world we live in. Knew it since the war. Poisoning our boys in those trenches. My nephew Tommy went off to war and never came back. That's when I knew we was going to hell. Right in a hand-basket."

Violet sipped her tea, enjoying Cook's tirade even if she muttered about how spoiled Victor was and how Violet and Mrs. Davies coddled him.

"Girls are never coddled, are they? The weaker sex. Weaker? You see a girl like Miss Meredith looking after her sister's little 'uns and not even saying a word against it. You see you, Miss Violet, looking after your brother. You think we don't see how he has his man, Giles, and you without a maid. Beatrice says you're looking after his room even now with us about to help you. Girls are never coddled. We just carry on. Struggling, working, having babies, taking care of our men. From the day it all begins 'til the day we die."

Violet pulled out her scrap of names and showed it to Hargreaves, who glanced it over.

"I don't believe Mr. Kingsley Allyn believed he'd inherit, Miss Violet. Your aunt was pretty blunt with him time and again."

"The police think he might have killed Aunt Agatha because he lost everything."

"I can't say if he did or not, miss. Only that he knew he wasn't in the will. It was always about you five young ones."

"Was it?"

Hargreaves and Cook both nodded.

"Uncle Kingsley knew it?"

They nodded again.

CHAPTER TWENTY-ONE

$\mathcal{V}$iolet left the kitchens before she made the servants uncomfortable with her presence. The five cousins who'd spent so much of their childhood with Aunt Agatha rattled around in Violet's mind. The five who'd been half-raised by Aunt Agatha and half-educated by her. The five listed in the will.

Violet removed herself, Victor, and John from the list of suspects and debated on Meredith and Algie. Her cousin, Algernon Allyn was spoiled, a bit thick, and prone to taking the easy way out. That was part of the problem wasn't it? He was an out and out dunce.

Violet could believe that he might cut a saddle girth in a moment of rage or push his aunt from a bridge if he'd been turned down or threatened to be cut from the will. Attempt after attempt? Grease on the stairs? That was more creative than Violet could justly give Algernon credit for. Maybe if Uncle Kingsley had been directing it all.

If, however, you were to look at just the five of them. What about Meredith? Her life was a nightmare. She had no relief in sight. She couldn't just marry for money like Algie. She couldn't just get a job like Algie. She couldn't use her connections for anything. Her connections had led her to a life of unpaid servitude.

She might have been told by Aunt Agatha to keep the faith. What if your life was miserable? What if it were just awful and you knew that a slight push of a woman off of a bridge or a small glass of sherry was all that stood between you and freedom. Would you kill then?

Violet's journey up the stairs was almost blind. The grease on the stairs was such a woman thing to do. Perhaps Algie would shove someone down the stairs, but he wouldn't grease them. Perhaps Algie would stab their aunt in the back, but he wouldn't think ahead, unlock the window, crawl through it, and...that wasn't something you could do without being seen.

If you were small enough, however, you could slip in and hide in the curtains and just...wait. You wouldn't even have to go through the window if you placed yourself behind the curtains and were patient.

A sudden memory crossed Violet's mind and with it, she was sure. Utterly sure. She passed Uncle Kingsley's room again and saw the constables searching. What were they looking for?

Poison? Muddied shoes from the flower bed? What if just on the side of the door, were a few pieces of evidence? What if Meredith was figuring a way to hide them while the police focused on the wrong relative? What if it was already too late?

Violet passed her own bedroom, her friends' rooms, her brother's space and made her way to the end of the hall. Meredith's bedroom was one of the smaller ones on this floor, but it had a beautiful view of the garden. Violet passed the room and walked down the servant stairs. They came out very near the door to the gardens only a few doors down from Aunt Agatha's office.

Any of the five cousins could have taken those stairs to the office, but Meredith's room was but a few steps from the servant case. Meredith would know when the servants were likely to be on the stair and when they'd be clear. Violet bet Algernon wouldn't have a clue about such things.

Violet slowly walked back up and stared at her cousin's door. Would it be so bad to search it? Perhaps. But Violet was going to anyway. She knocked on the door. There was no answer.

She knocked again and carefully called, "Meredith, love? Are you in there?"

The was no reply. Slowly, Violet twisted the doorknob and stepped inside. She glanced quickly around and found it empty. Violet breathed slowly out. The bed was made, and Meredith's small trunk was in the corner of the room, closed.

Violet crossed to the trunk and opened it. There was nothing inside. The wish of a small vial or packet that could have been used for arsenic burned away in the light of emptiness. Violet pushed herself to her feet, crossed to the bed and glanced underneath. Not even dust under the bed.

On the desk, there was a start of a letter to Meredith's mother. It didn't say anything useful such as 'I've successfully murdered Aunt Agatha and can now afford to escape Gertrude's demon children.'

Violet opened the wardrobe and found three dresses. Meredith's coat and hat were carefully hung up. A single pair of stockings and a few unmentionables were in the drawer of the wardrobe.

Violet sighed. Nothing. She had been foolish to look. Perhaps the police had already searched. So easy to find nothing when there was nothing to be found.

The door of the bedroom opened and Violet spun around. She met Meredith's gaze.

"Whatever are you doing in here, cousin?" Meredith asked. Her gaze had changed from the usual cold distance to something different. Something scary.

Violet considered and then decided to risk her thoughts out in the open. "It was you."

Meredith laughed and then her gaze narrowed on Violet.

"It was you," Meredith countered with a small smile about her lips. "You're the one who inherited the most. All I got was an allowance. Almost nothing compared to your heaps."

"She told you that you would get it, didn't she? Something to help you hold on through the hard times. Aunt Agatha saw how tired you were from caring for your sister's children and the way your family treats you, and she promised a better future."

Meredith's mouth twisted and she said, "A better future? No."

"Cook remembers," Violet lied. "She remembers that you perked up after the lawyer came and Aunt Agatha changed her will. Did she take you out of it after you married your husband and he lost everything? That seems like something she would do. We were being tested all our lives and didn't even know it. I bet you failed when you let your husband lose everything you had. Did you show up dejected and broken and play on her unwarranted love for you?"

Meredith stepped precisely into her room. It didn't have two comfortable chairs next to the fire like Violet's, but Meredith perched on the end of the bed. "Fairy stories and attempts to slide out of the mess you've made."

"You saw me with the letter opener in my hand."

Beatrice appeared in the doorway for a moment and then stepped to the side. Violet was certain that the girl was still there on the other side of the doorway. Reliable, wonderful Beatrice.

"Nonsense and fairy stories."

"You knew I was the main heir. Hargreaves saw you eavesdropping with the lawyer." That was a wild guess, but Violet had seen Meredith eavesdrop more than once herself. "Aunt Agatha told you that she'd fix the will after she saw you. She changed it and you listened to find out what you'd receive. It wasn't fair, but it was enough."

Meredith paused, momentarily at a loss for words and Violet was *certain*.

"Hargreaves saw you. You're the only one who could easily reach the house for the early attempts on her life. Victor and I took the train to Shelby. We met your demon twins. We talked to your sister. I wouldn't have blamed you for getting away if you'd just found a job. Your sister is terrible. It's a new age for women, Merry. There was no need to murder to escape your lot. We even have the vote."

"A new age? So I could share a room in London with other working girls? Living like sardines in a can, slaving away as a typist for some animal who thinks it's acceptable to manhandle me? I don't think so. Why is it fair that you and Victor have everything? You were already well set up when she left you *everything*."

Violet swallowed her shout of fury before she said, "So you pondered on how you were in the will. You remembered how—even if it wasn't as much as I received—that it would get you away from your sister."

"And punish you! You aren't better than me. You weren't more attentive. You were awful. You and Victor pulled pranks and caused trouble. I was an *angel!* I listened. I did everything I could to get Aunt Agatha to love me, and she never did!"

Violet closed her eyes for a moment and then said, "You didn't love her."

Meredith's mouth slowly opened and she sputtered.

"She wasn't stupid, Meredith. Aunt Agatha knew you didn't love her. Algie was *fond* of the old girl. John cared for her, but didn't make her a priority. You want to know why I was favored? I loved her. I needed her. Victor loved her too."

"They won't believe Hargreaves over me. He's a servant. He's nothing."

"They'll be able to track down the cyanide now that they know where to look. The problem with so many attempts on her life that failed was that there were so many chances to catch you. It won't take them long to find the proof."

Meredith gasped and jumped to her feet. Fate seemed to be mocking her and she shrieked in fury, lunging at Violet and shoving her. Violet had no warning. Trading polite accusations and then she was falling back. She tripped on the brick near the fireplace and hit the ground. Pain rushed her leg, and Violet screamed.

Meredith darted out as Beatrice rushed in.

"Miss Violet!" Beatrice shouted. "Help!"

Beatrice beat at Violet's dress, crying as she did. It took Violet too long to realize that she had been on fire. By Jove, she had been on fire.

Vi sat up and looked at her leg. The fire hadn't extended beyond her dress. The pain had stopped. More pain from heat than from fire burning her legs. She was all right.

"Thank you," Violet whispered to Beatrice, remembering again that nothing was right for Aunt Agatha.

Tears started to fall and Beatrice pulled Violet close, hugging her tightly. "There, there," Beatrice said. "There, there."

"Oh," Violet breathed. "Oh." She pulled away and looked up at the kneeling Beatrice. "I..."

A realization of what had happened seemed to occur to them both at the same time.

"She...she...killed Mrs. Davies!"

"Go tell Mr. Wakefield," Violet said. "Quickly now. They have to catch her."

CHAPTER TWENTY-TWO

$\mathcal{M}$eredith didn't make it farther than the long drive to Aunt Agatha's house when the constables found her. They put Meredith in the back of their auto and drove her to the police station before the rumors of what she had done had flown through the house.

Jack Wakefield followed while Victor raged over the sight of Violet's burned dress. Lila and Gwennie bundled Violet into a bath and a nightgown. It took a stiff whiskey, two gin rickeys, and Beatrice holding Violet's hand until she was able to calm down enough to sleep. Even then, she cried while she slept.

The sun was high in the sky and the servants busy when Violet woke the next day. Beatrice was near at hand and disappeared the moment Violet sat up, returning with Giles's famous and effective morning after remedy, two pills, and a tea tray.

"Bless you," Violet said. She moved slowly through her ablutions until Victor appeared.

"Come on now, luv." His voice was gentle. "You need more than toast, and Mr. Coates needs to speak with us."

Violet followed her brother down the stairs and into the yellow room. She didn't really listen until a rather large number broke through her fog.

"I don't understand," Violet said. "How much?"

Mr. Coates repeated the amount and Violet choked. He gazed at her a few minutes while she drank tea and stared at the wall. Finally her gaze turned to Victor who seemed as shocked as she was.

"I didn't realize the old girl had succeeded quite so well at her game," he said.

Neither had Violet. She hadn't the faintest clue.

"I..." She paused, closed her eyes, and said, "I need you to pay off Uncle Kingsley's debts. Enough to keep him out of debtor's prison. The same for Algernon. Pay off his debt and make sure he's aware that we won't do it again."

Mr. Coates' expression said what he thought of those endeavors, but Violet just couldn't allow her uncle to suffer when she'd been given so much. They signed papers while Victor paced in the background. He hadn't been surprised by what Violet had requested for her uncle, and he wouldn't be surprised when she escaped the yellow room before she heard more. She didn't want the money, she wanted her aunt.

"Victor," Violet said, cutting into Mr. Coates commentary. "I want to go."

"Paris?"

She nodded. He could have said anything, and she'd have said yes.

"No," he suggested, "it's so grey in Paris during the holidays. Let's skip Paris and go straight to Italy."

That was fine, too. She didn't care. She just needed to leave the place where her aunt, the only mother she clearly remembered, had been stolen from her. Violet made her way to her rooms and packed her bags. They could leave first thing in the morning.

That evening, Jack Wakefield found her as she sat in Aunt Agatha's library. She was alone, though Victor and their friends had *checked* on her several times. She looked up expecting her twin and found Jack Wakefield.

"I am leaving in the morning," Jack said. "Father is well enough to leave his room and doesn't want to stay where his friend was stolen from him."

A feeling Violet understood all too well. "Victor and I are going as well."

"Paris?"

"The Amalfi coast."

Jack nodded. He made no other comment on her destination but she hoped that light she saw in his gaze was approval. He slowly took her hand. "There is much to do for your aunt even now. I will see her through to justice."

Violet nodded. She didn't know what to say. She stared down where his large hand engulfed hers. Once again, the feeling of being small next to his bulk struck her. Once again, she discovered that she enjoyed that feeling. He made her feel both safe and so very womanly.

"You will be seeing me again, Lady Violet Carlyle."

Her gaze jerked up to his and she nodded almost helplessly.

"Until then." He squeezed her hand once and was gone before she recovered from his unexpected promise.

"Miss?"

Violet turned from the view of the sea to Beatrice. The maid had a bit of a tan and a smile that brightened the greyest of days.

"Mr. Victor has returned."

He'd gone to town to purchase something. Had it been a painting? She thought it might be. Something for his office when they returned home. The weeks since losing her aunt and gaining an inheritance had been long. There was something about the sun and the wind that had made them bearable.

"He has a letter from home and would like you to join him."

Violet followed Beatrice down to the little table on the back patio that overlooked the sea. Victor sipped something while Lila and Gwennie leaned back, eyes closed under the warmth of the sun. It didn't matter that it was January and wasn't all that warm. It was just that it was so beautiful.

"How are you, luv?"

She smiled and perhaps for the first time since losing her aunt, Violet was able to answer honestly, "I am well."

"We've been called home."

Violet considered. No longer were they reliant on the income from their father. While they'd been here, Hargreaves had been packing the things Aunt Agatha had left them in the big house and moving it all to London for their return. They didn't have to go anywhere they didn't wish. They could say no. Freedom had never been more free with so much money at their fingertips.

"Isolde is getting married."

"Oh, no," Violet laughed, shocked at her genuine humor. "Now no one will ever want to marry me. Once your younger sister is wed, all chances of love have been frittered away."

"That wasn't true," Lila laughed, "even before you started swimming in the green. Now, my luv, everyone knows what a catch you are."

"Drowning in the green," Victor added, "our Violet. Drowning in money. A terrible fate."

"Smothered by it," Gwennie added with a laugh. "If only we were all so encumbered."

"I wouldn't mind returning to my poor working Denny," Lila said. "Gwennie wouldn't mind stumbling across Mr. John Davies. You wouldn't mind running into your Mr. Wakefield."

"I wouldn't mind," Victor said, "watching Lady Eleanor attempt to cozy up to us now that we're cronies with Midas."

Violet smiled. The sea was beautiful this time of year, but it would be better in the summer.

"I wouldn't mind," Violet announced, "those things myself."

THE END

ALSO BY BETH BYERS

The Violet Carlyle Mysteries

Murder & The Heir

Murder at Kennington House

Murder at the Folly

A Merry Little Murder

*New Year's Madness (a short story collection)

*Valentine's Madness (a short story collection)

Murder Among the Roses

Murder in the Shallows

Gin & Murder

Obsidian Murder

Murder at the Ladies Club

Wedding Vows & Murder

The 2nd Chance Diner Mysteries

Spaghetti, Meatballs, & Murder

Cookies & Catastrophe

(found in the Christmas boxset, The Three Carols of Cozy Christmas Murder)

Poison & Pie

Double Mocha Murder

Cinnamon Rolls & Cyanide

Tea & Temptation

Donuts & Danger

Scones & Scandal

Lemonade & Loathing

Wedding Cake & Woe

Honeymoons & Honeydew

The Pumpkin Problem

The Brightwater Bay Mysteries

(co-written with Carolyn L. Dean and Angela Blackmoore)

A Little Taste of Murder

(found in the Christmas boxset, The Three Carols of Cozy Christmas Murder)

A Tiny Dash of Death

A Sweet Spoonful of Cyanide

ALSO BY AMANDA A. ALLEN

The Mystic Cove Mommy Mysteries

Bedtimes & Broomsticks
Runes & Roller Skates
Costumes and Cauldrons (found in the anthology Witch or Treat)
Banshees and Babysitters
Spellbooks and Sleepovers: A Mystic Cove Short Story
Hobgoblins and Homework
Gifts and Ghouls (found in the anthology Spells and Jinglebells)
Christmas and Curses
Potions & Passions (found in the anthology Hexes and Ohs)
Valentines & Valkyries
Infants & Incantations (Coming Soon)

The Rue Hallow Mysteries

Hungry Graves
Lonely Graves
Sisters and Graves

ALSO BY AMANDA A. ALLEN

Yule Graves
Fated Graves
Ruby Graves

AUTHOR'S NOTE

I just need to take a few minutes to thank my wonderful editors C. Jane Reid, Bonnie Brien, and Erin Lynn.

Further gratitude goes to my little ones. There really aren't words enough to say how patient my kids are with me when I'm in book crunch zone. They're fabulous, and I'm lucky to be their Mom. Noah, Olivia, Isabella, Benjamin—you are everything in the world to me and why I work hard.

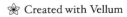

Made in the USA
Middletown, DE
01 July 2019